The Bay of Silence

Lisa St Aubin de Terán was born in London in 1953. At the age of sixteen she left James Allen's Girls' School to marry. She and her exiled Venezuelan husband travelled for two years in Italy before returning to his family home in the Andes. After seven years, during which she managed her husband's sugar plantation and avocado farm, she came back to England with her daughter and now lives in Norfolk. *Keepers of the House* is her first novel and won a Somerset Maugham Award in 1983. A second, *The Slow Train to Milan,* won the John Llewelyn Rhys Memorial Prize for 1983, and a third is entitled *The Tiger*.

Lisa St Aubin de Terán

The Bay of Silence

Pavanne
Published by Pan Books

First published 1986 by Jonathan Cape Ltd
This Pavanne edition published 1987 by Pan Books Ltd,
Cavaye Place, London, SW10 9PG
9 8 7 6 5 4 3 2 1
© Lisa St Aubin de Terán 1986
ISBN 0 330 29884 4

Printed and bound in Great Britain by
Richard Clay Ltd, Bungay, Suffolk

For George MacBeth

CONTENTS

I

William

They call it the two-faced place in Genovese, and they are wary of its people. It straggles down a small promontory and then falls away on either side into the sea. On one side of the peninsula a wide bay of black sand fringed by cypress and palms meets the road and railway tunnels blasted out of solid rock. This is the bay that Hans Christian Anderson called the Bay of Fairytales. On the other side, a series of slipways leads off the narrow high street on to a crescent of faded stuccoed villas whose backs rise out of the fine yellow sand of the Bay of Silence. A Capuchin monastery crouches above this mysteriously calm bay, and its balustraded gardens climb the steep wooded slopes of the mainland. There is a sense of time held in suspension here, and but for pigeons scouring the beach, it is usually deserted. These are the two faces of Sestri Levante, to which the wealthy Genovese have been coming since it was a plain fishing village gilded by both the rising and the setting sun.

We came here first for our honeymoon, thirteen years ago. It was your choice then, but I never regretted it. This time round, I remembered the place and brought you back here, to this strange haven on the Italian Riviera. We hardly ever talk about our honeymoon, maybe that is normal, maybe other couples don't, but there was the first hint of something wrong even then, and sometimes it was much more than a hint. You were twenty, and glamorous, with five years of big films already behind you. I was just an unknown graphic designer.

I never knew myself, why you chose me, and clung, and filled and drained me until we became what we are: two people hiding the

9

world from each other. I've been driven here by my paranoia, and by that slow dread of what will happen to you, to me, to the girls, if anyone finds out about Amadeo, our dead baby. I miss him, Rosalind, and I shudder when I remember what happened out there on the other sands, in France. So I sit here in Sestri Levante, trying to piece together what we have done wrong. And I watch you, Rosalind, as you watch the sea, and it frightens me.

It was always my father who most used to frighten me – the Reverend Walsh from the Norfolk fens. He would certainly have advised me now to start at the beginning. He was a man who never suffered from doubts, either on his own account or on that of others. He knew what was right and wrong, and where a beginning began and where a story had to end. If he could see me trying to reconstruct this story of two people, that is, of you, Rosalind, and me, he would tell me to begin with our respective childhoods and then move on from there. But to go back, in my case to that bleak rectory and my mother's unforgiving smiles, would be premature. And it would be too soon to go back, in your case, to the day when they found you, aged eleven, in bed with your Uncle Bertie. I want to start with what I know, not what your parents or mine have told me. There'll be time enough for all the things we ought to know, later.

So I'll start with Sestri Levante, and our honeymoon at the Hotel Paradiso, and the time which you said was the happiest of your life. If you were to ask me why I need to go over the details of these past years, I can only say that I want to get to the other side of you – to be a part of it, to break through that daydream of yours or at least reach into it – and, I suppose, just that I love you. If, instead of my talking to the twilight and the slow waves lapping on the orange-cartons on the shore, you were to be here beside me on this slatted bench, I would feel calmer. I always feel better when you're physically near. I can't even get properly worried when I'm with you. You get so bored by the talk of love. But then some things do bore you, nowadays.

I remember that we arrived here that first time by car. I'd hired it at the seedy airport at Genova, and driven the short way along the coast past Rapallo and Chiavari and through the tunnel to the peninsula of Sestri itself. By that time I was a wreck. Everything I had ever heard about Italian driving was an understatement; and I realized, as we sliced our way between the cliff edge and the rock face, swerving with what turned out to be inspired desperation, that there are elements of manic driving that just can't be put into words. You said it was like the films, the old ones, not the ones you'd been in. For me, it was like all the bad rides in all the worst funfairs I'd ever been to; and a kind of masochism had taken me to a lot. I was sick in the pit of my stomach, out there, in that green convertible. Half the time I wasn't aware of the car at all, just of the precipice and my nerves, and things coming at us at incredible speeds from dim-lit tunnels. I made a mental note not to drive again, at least not on the Riviera. And if, in London, I took the 24 bus from South End Green to the West End with monotonous regularity, leaving our own car to gather dust and chewing gum by the kerb, perhaps it owed something to that mad drive of ours. In my memory the brakes failed, chickens and dogs were slain, and I had to race to stay alive. I don't know why I drove so fast, perhaps it was some kind of contagious frenzy, a foretaste of that Mediterranean hysteria one hears so much about, or just misplaced machismo. Whatever it was, we arrived, and supervised the unloading of our luggage: my one bag, and your fleet of matching leather cases. Even in those days you travelled with an inanimate entourage, as though there were some security in numbers, numbers of anything, luggage, friends, lovers.

I remember our arrival at the hotel less clearly than all that happened afterwards, perhaps because it was the one event untainted by anything disturbing. Or maybe it was just because my legs were still trembling from the drive. Milton, your agent, claims that I am a glutton for punishment, and so I am, in some ways, my mother made sure of that, but a man can go so far and no further even in the pursuit of nostalgia. So this time round we are lodged not at the Paradiso but on the Bay of Silence itself. I have thought of going round to our old hotel, which is a mere stroll from us now. I pass it daily on my Sestrian patrol down the Corso Colombo with its quaint twists and shops. Then I hairpin round to the heavy evergreens of the piazza, with only a cursory obeisance to the sea front on the wider beach, before turning back to the other side and our bay. However, when I pass the terrace and the main door to the Paradiso, I get a sense almost of sacrilege. When I push my thoughts further, I imagine that long-lost and soiled underpants will fall out of cupboards if I open them there, and stray, unaccounted-for feet will step out from behind doors. I convinced myself weeks ago, though, that it wasn't worth the emotional hassle of going back in, so I haven't. But I can't imagine it has really changed, given that the wishing-fountain is still outside, and the church bells still toll interminably opposite. I see that the group of old men, as planted by the Italian Tourist Board, still sits in the small piazza in the evenings mending their fishing nets under the setting sun, with their gnarled hands hauling the nets across to the stone fountain. Even without such sights, an afternoon in Sestri Levante suffices to discover the double nature of the place: the back to backing of the trendy and the ancient, of wealth and poverty, of ritual and decadence. Sestri Levante thrives on its duality, and anyone who comes, however tormented by his own nature, will be soothed by its blatant schizophrenia.

It may seem naïve of me to say so now, but I didn't know that you were schizophrenic when I married you. I hasten to say that I wouldn't have loved you any less if I *had* known, it is just that it is nice to know things. I suppose it is reassuring, like having one's days numbered to three score and ten, or getting an exam result. I could see that you were different, but then it didn't take a Ph.D. to do so. You were beautiful, strange, dreamy and withdrawn. I thought you were wonderful – I still do, and now I know that there are two of you, neither one of you baffles or hurts me quite as much as you used to.

Sometimes, at a dinner, I used to get a sinking feeling that my neighbour was rambling on with no apparent end, and a kind of hopelessness turned me off my food. I have observed, in my amateur way, that the offending rambler did not notice himself being boring until considerably later, if ever. I think that is what I am doing now.

The sea is getting rough again tonight. Every time I try to conjure up a picture of the Hotel Paradiso in my mind's eye sufficient to describe it, I see you, Rosalind, with your Pre-Raphaelite tawny hair. You never like being called blonde. I remember how you used to come down like a mallet on any reporter who described you as 'a blonde'. I keep needing to see you, again and again. I used to tell myself to 'make the most of it', a bit of sound advice for my youth sort of thing, and then it would all calm down. It doesn't grow calm, though, if anything it gets worse, but lulls come now, short ones, but still lulls. I congratulate myself on my new-found freedom and I put my scattered emotions back in their cigarette carton and promise myself to be a better man. And then . . . back to idiocy and adolescent panic and pre-adolescent despair. Which all goes to show that it is a dog's life: eating, sleeping and making love.

After we arrived, on that first evening and made a simulacrum of settling in to our room – we had come for six weeks – we had a late siesta. We had a room with windows on two sides. We were neither of us novices at making love, at that time; I flatter myself that I had been with many more lovers than you, making up, I suppose, for the lost love of my childhood. I didn't mean that wrongly, in view of what happened in yours, just that I never had any real love at home or any physical contact. My mother referred to sex (and only when it was quite unavoidable) as 'all that' and she found it utterly distasteful. She also managed to include under this general label of 'all that sort of thing' kissing and cuddling and holding hands. So we never did, at home. There was never a hair stroked or an arm touched at the rectory. Later, when I got away to London, the sin city itself, I found my own sensuality. Then, eventually, at the brazen age of twenty-six, I found you, my perfect mate. Though I had had more lovers by far before we met, I know that you have 'caught up' as it were after our marriage, and probably, for all I know, far surpassed my bachelor tally. But if I close my eyes, Rosalind, and become suddenly innumerate, you are still mine, and that is how I like to see you sometimes, feeling that what you give to me specifically you give to no one else.

In the early days, during our brief engagement, and on the honeymoon, I thought you were giving me everything. You seemed so happy, and I felt so good, and I spent more hours inside you than any working man could (I was freelance by then). Something very special began that day, in Italy after the suicide drive, the hours of lovemaking, and then the tremendous chiming of the church bells outside that so startled you that you nearly fell out of bed. It was seven o'clock. We didn't know then the significance of that chiming,

13

just that the bells tolled and echoed and made the shutters rattle and the walls shake like an imminent earthquake in our room. They were only a few yards away, clanging relentlessly in their massive tower at the populace of that small town who had grown not to heed them. There was a terrible urgency in their sound. Later we thought that it was the old Sestri appealing to the new from the dock. Or else it was the death toll of the old town calling the new to mourn and being refused and so tolling louder, tolling so that just the sound itself would be dirge enough for an outcrop of rock in the sea with a church and a castle and a personality problem.

It was dark when we went out, it was March and the evenings were short. You had a glow on your face and a kind of inner smile. Very rarely on the screen had the camera caught that special smile of yours, and then never entirely. Despite your success, your real talent couldn't ever be confined, or distilled. It was as though the world was your set, and there were no cuts, no editing, just a work of living art unravelling, with all the barriers of reality removed. That was what it was like on that first night when we walked across the flat-cobbled street to the gap in the walls that led down to the Bay of Silence. The church bells had stopped ringing but they had left in their wake a feel of religiosity. It was like my father's church after the service was over and all the parishioners had gone. I would be left standing alone, often hiding, under the arch of twelfth-century beams curving into stone. I used to feel that a spirit was up there somewhere, if only I could break through the cant and hypocisy and the tight-mouthed lip service.

We walked down the sandy alleyway for the few feet that separated the town from the hidden beach, and then we were on the sand, looking out across a small harbour banked up with rock where it opened to the sea. Along its three sides, villas rose up in gracious stuccoes, and looked noble even in their slight dilapidation. There were a few fishing boats dragged on to the beach, and one or two left bobbing in the shallow waters. Electric lights from some of the houses and occasional street lights curving up the hill played havoc with the natural shadows of the moon on the water. They seemed to focus on one point, like a theatre light on the prima donna, on the spot on the water where there was a golden dazzle. We stood and stared, and as our eyes grew used to the dark, I saw what you had obviously already seen – a boy with eyes more beautiful than seemed possible. He was more beautiful even than you. He seemed quite unreal, standing Christlike on his think boat on the water, returning our stare.

When I say Christlike it was his apparent standing on the waves and the power that he held over us, over you, that I refer to. He bore no resemblance to the man in the pictures at my Sunday school or in any of the books and leaflets distributed there. Although I call him a boy, he was probably just a bit younger than myself. His name turned out to be Angelo, which I confess grated a little on me. You took it as an instant confirmation of his divinity.

I have often wondered if you would have been as enthralled if instead of Angelo, your angel's name had turned out to be Reinaldo or Umberto or something even less mystical. Names in themselves are very strange. Take William, for example. Being called William in the impoverished fringes of upper-class England is arguably worse for a boy than being called Sue. I know, of course, that is a fine name, famed and flaunted by kings and warriors since earliest times. However, in a country where a spade is called a spade and a cock a willie, the sexual overtones of the name are never far away. They were never nearer than in Waddesford Manor Private Boarding School for the sons of the clergy.

Life became a matter of survival. At the age of thirteen I learnt three important new things. Firstly, I learnt that rock bottom is always lower than you think. I thought my parents were the most narrow-minded, strict and antiquated relics left in the Church of England. I was wrong. There were boys who came from homes that made our austere rectory look like an amusement arcade. Then, in the traumatic corridors with their combined atmosphere of menace and spite, I discovered that home was still home, however horrible it was, with the ghetto-like safety of familiarity, at least. Lastly, and rather more brutally, I discovered that I, William Walsh, was to be the laughing-stock and sexual butt of almost the entire school, and all because of my Christian name. Particularly in my first year, the boys were very unChristian about it.

I don't know how it 'got out' on that first day. I still didn't know some boys' names after my first summer term there. Yet somehow, one of the seniors got hold of the lists and discovered the awful truth. Then the teasing and bullying began and continued unchecked until in my third year I broke Anderson major's nose in an inspired fluke punch that put an end to my torment. The good thing about a school like Waddesford Manor is that once you've survived it, you feel you can survive anything. Then, by comparison, everything is bliss: beds, food, baths, even other people. I still think it's a wonder that my own tender willie survived the abuse and the pulling and taunting to go on to have any kind of happy heterosexual life. So much for my own wonders and their sordid origins, you had your own one there, your Angelo, with his halo of pale gold curls and his startling bright eyes and his face chiselled as from some dark marble.

I don't know how you met later, or what was said or done. I know that when the bells chimed every evening at seven, you would rise from wherever you were and go towards the bay, and be gone sometimes for hours. And I know that in the night sometimes, when I awoke still exhausted from making love you would be gone from your bed. Through the half-haze of my dreams I would see you come back, dishevelled, with that wild dreamy look in your eye. And you would cling to me, and want to make love again and again and only then would you sleep a little, that sex-drugged sleep of yours. I know that all through the day, every day, you would be aware of the trains passing through the rock tunnel into Sestri station some distance away. You could hear the whistles blowing from across the big bay, and you knew, I thought then as if by magic, the names and the destinations of those trains.

You would pause in the middle of lunch, with your tagliatelle a la carbonara poised in mid-air, and hearing the distant rumble you would say, 'That's the 12.35 to Milan.'

It was as though the whole railway network were linked to your arteries, and with each freight or express train that came and went, a new surge of blood passed through to your brain. When they were late, you seemed to suffer some physical pain, a kind of nervous migraine. I came to know that timetable too, by proxy, so when you winced and left your afternoon tea untouched, I knew even before you told me that the Roma Express was late.

There was a board in the station to the left of the ticket office, with every departure and arrival marked up on it. I thought perhaps that was where you went to. I went there myself sometimes, under the guise of buying an English newspaper or a packet of tissues or a cheap romantic novel, but I never saw you there. After about two weeks of your disappearance, in a fit of sudden jealousy or concern, I walked all round the Bay of Silence, and discovered that small alleyways led in and out of it to the rest of the town. After that, it disturbed me more when you went away at the seven o'clock times. Until then, I had been able to reassure myself that you were merely brooding by the water, reliving the religious feeling of your first night. And even though I once followed you there and saw you waiting by the waterside, lost in thought, I felt that you could be anywhere.

On a further foray into the town, I found a sinister passageway, or *sottopassaggio,* which led under the railway tracks to the other side of town. This was a part of Sestri Levante that I didn't know existed until that day. There seemed to be more than enough to contend with on our side of the tracks without this new part, which was scarcely new at all, straggling into the hills and out of my grasp.

One evening, coming down the balustraded slope on the far side of your bay, I call it yours because you made it your own, and drained some magic from it that was inaccessible to me, I saw you in the distance. I never confronted you about it – what was there to say? You were lying in a deep boat just off the shore, I recognized your bare back and your hair and Angelo's hair. You were lying on top of him. It was forty-five minutes exactly since you had been doing the same to me. If I hadn't been up there, on the hill, I couldn't have seen. Even under those circumstances your back looked lovely. You used to say that you had the most lovely spine in the Western Hemisphere, and I believe you have. When we were out together, or at parties, and the photographers flocked round you, you used to turn your back on them, and if they complained, that's what you'd say, 'This is the most lovely back in the Western Hemisphere.'

I wanted to feel angry and cheated. I wanted to be able to shout at you when you came back, or just be really silent and hurt. But I couldn't do it, Rosalind, I just wanted you, wanted to run my fingers down your back, and see you there with me. What was one time? One lapse in a rowing boat? So I did what you do, Rosalind, I

17

pretended I hadn't seen, that it hadn't happened, that there was no Angelo sharing you with me. Then you came back to the Paradiso, and ran up the stairs breathlessly, and flung yourself down on our bed and asked for me, just as you had done so many evenings before. That was the only thing that upset me, that you should return so ready, because then I wondered if all the other times, too, you came from another man to me, as fragile and resilient as a ping-pong ball, prey to any capricious batting, the original shuttle-cock.

What we had, though, was too good to lose by a word or look, and so I readjusted the scene, made the boat smaller, made you sleep in my new dream, took Angelo out from under you and replaced him with fishing nets. Even in moments of seriousness, it's impossible to control one's mind entirely. So as I put the fishing nets in the boat, and had you mend them face down in the sun, I was struck by the image of an English country house and of the well-known tale of the hostess coming round, showing off her home to a group of young girls who had arrived for a weekend houseparty, and on opening the door to a particular drawing-room and finding two guests fornicating on the floor had said without a moment's hesitation, by way of explanation to her baffled and innocent charges, 'Oh, they're mending the carpet, how kind!' So I had to re-edit even the new version and take out the fishing nets, too redolent of sex and carpets, and just have you sunbathing on your own.

I never really minded the layers of your deceit, I had my own, and knew that they were mostly innocent. Mine went back to my child-hood, as I'm sure yours did, and they were just my way of surviving the probing, and the unsympathetic surroundings I was forced to spend so much time in. Even in a court of law, self-defence is no crime. I didn't know why you did what you did, or even, to be honest, what it was that you did. Basically, though, you were a 'good sort' and I believed sincerely that you loved me, and you could do no wrong for me. You were always my vision, my winged messenger of another world. When once, in a state of maudlin appreciation, I had told you this before our marraige, you insisted that there were no women angels, only men. The four archangels and all their hosts, from Sariel, the choirmaster, to Samuel, the angel of death, were male. So, I thought, you had bridged that gap.

Occasionally when I see my own eyes I get worried. Our respective vanity is like an undercurrent, I sometimes think, keeping us in the same drag if not on the same wave. My eyes are blue, yours are a clear and deeply disturbing grey. The only other people I've ever seen with such clear or such beautiful eyes as yours were Angelo and Amadeo. I see their eyes so often in my mind like the eyes of seagulls, or the drowned eyes of shipwrecked sailors, as mysterious as the sea itself.

I wonder if I am really any nearer to knowing you after peeling off all these layers of years than when I first met you. Now you're thirty-three, trapped in a dream, mother of twin girls more capricious and wild than you ever were yourself, and of a dead son and a host of memories that haunt you. Some things never seem to change, though. When I first met you, it was my Jimmy who made you laugh, and he can still make you laugh at any time. You ask for him as though he were a real person separate from myself, just as you ask for others of my repertoire, the United supporter and the cabbie and the Anglican vicar. Perhaps that's another reason why you need me so much, because I am more than myself. So when you ask for Jimmy, a fully fledged Italian waiter emerges from my mouth. I've noticed that you'll say things to this Jimmy that you wouldn't say to me, but most of all, you'll laugh.

I love being with you, Rosalind, but I can't seem to laugh much any more. It's as though my mouth has tightened as my mother's mouth did at some time, long before I was born, I'm sure. I would do anything to relax, anything. But I have this dread inside me, about you, about what could happen to you if anything went wrong again. Nobody would understand that you didn't mean any harm, and that you have really never done anything bad. Everything that happened happened by accident, and you just are the way you are: reshaping reality when it intrudes too far. I know that, and I believe in you, but would anyone else? Would they give you the benefit of the doubt? Or would they begin to unearth and unravel all the years of unthinking and hold them against you and drag you down with the dirt that is really no part of you? Even when I'm asleep, I feel that I'm not sleeping, and when I'm awake my eyes ache from worrying like this. I imagine that someone will see a colour sign, that a stranger will denounce us, that a rash word of yours will give you away.

And the wretched fish shop, with its trays of slime, always has a basket of crabs in one corner, and you know that's the one thing I can't bear to see. You've made yourself forget the reason why, and you take it just as an eccentricity of mine, a quirk to be indulged. I have heard you tell people, 'Willie hates crabs.' As you might announce that one of our daughters hates tapioca.

It doesn't do to get too tragic about these things, I know. I suppose I have a tendency to feel sad. My mother had a way of dampening enthusiasm of any kind with the mock sympathy of the phrase, 'Oh dear, what a pity!' All the good things and the bad were levelled by that common denominator; my early pictures, books, the thrill of new friends, special presents for her own unwanting hands were all met with that same grim smile. I don't know what made my mother so bitter; whether it was the war or my father or the genteel poverty of her married years, or the bleak and numbing isolation of the Norfolk fens. Maybe it was just the dreadful smell of paraffin clinging to everything and still not keeping out the East wind cold. I suppose she felt she had to try with me, it was her duty, but I used to think that she didn't know how harsh she was to me. Then, after she died, I got a letter from her bank, typically. She told me in it that she hoped I would forgive her for her hardness and the lack of love that she'd always shown to me, but that something had happened long ago that had turned her heart to pumice stone. She said, as well, that she'd often seen herself with me, and wished that she could have been otherwise. The idea of my mother having both a heart and a soul, of whatever substance, was astounding, and my own pumiced memory has looked at her a little more kindly ever since.

What do you think about, Rosalind, when you stare at the sea? Perhaps it's better that I don't know. It soothes me now to look at the waves. I used to think it a bad thing that you stared out as you do, but now I know it's soothing. When we lived inland, you used to stare out of the window on to the unkept grass of the back garden and will the sea to be there, and then sit for hours consulting your imaginary waves. So the two sides of you relax, where I can't seem to, but I'm learning, apprenticed to the tides. I suppose if you had wanted to tell me what you were thinking, you would have done so long ago, or are you waiting for me to find out for myself?

II

Rosalind

The first time I ever really felt something completely, in the way that I thought life ought to be felt, was when I saw Angelo on the water. Before that, I had occasionally been on the brink of this experience – having orgasms, battling and winning at an auction, eating a really good chocolate cake – but I would always stop short and be left with nothing more than the almost immediate need to try again. Angelo pierced through all that. He gave me the strength to survive.

When a woman goes into a coma and lies unconscious for days and even weeks or months, doctors know now that the patient can hear what is being said around her. She can hear the nurses discussing her case, and their boyfriends and the matron; and through the haze, somewhere between life and death, she knows what is happening around her. So, too, a person's spirit can drift out of a bed or chair and watch that same person's body from a distance. These are accepted phenomena. The blind can hear the blind and the deaf can feel the deaf, but no one credits a person's duality as being normal. Thus, I am labelled a 'cured schizophrenic'. Let them label me, it's easier than arguing. Maybe, sometimes, a person really isn't aware of another being kept in her body and taking turns with her to do things. Or maybe, as in some ancestral feud, she chooses to ignore it. Or maybe, as in my case, life is easier when one side dominates the other and is better left that way, given that in all relationships one half must be led or everything would stand still. So I know, Willie Walsh and all the rest of you, that I'm twice what I seem to be and half of what I am, but so what?

Willie and I are like a couple bound by Superglue. We don't know what holds us together, apart from this special chemical agent that won't and can't let go. I believe there are recorded cases of surgical separation. As in the instance of the jealous wife who bound her sleeping husband's hand to his penis. Our embrace is, definitely, more intimate than that; and is surgery always advisable?

Willie wants to know my thoughts, the depths of my supposed insanity, but I'm not convinced he would love me so much if he knew them all or even if I would, if I talked that much to him. A woman has to have her secrets, it gives her a sense of power to know that there's always another layer to strip off, at will, and yet not do so. And then, very rarely, she'll let another veil fall, always to reveal one more, always one last veil before the end, and there being no end.

Willie's mother was an old cow, I don't often tell him this because he becomes protective about her memory. On the infrequent occasions when I met her, though – which were: twice at the rectory, pinned to my chair by marauding draughts and her would-be lethal stare, once for a disastrous tea in London, and a couple of times about the babies – we didn't get on. I thought that she should be drowned in a barrel of brine and would have happily volunteered to carry out the sentence. For her part, she made no effort to disguise the fact that she thought I was the most brazen strumpet ever to grow out of the United Kingdom, if not the world. All the time that she looked me up and down with prime disgust, which meant, in effect, all the time we were in the same room, I could see her weighing this point with herself; was it just to be Great Britain, or was it an international issue?

Our very first meeting, the one that set the tone for all the rest, took place in the damp drawing-room of the rectory where Willie grew up. To be quite fair to Willie, he had described the house and his mother with a wealth of grisly detail before he went. It was I who insisted on taking the glad tidings out to Norfolk in person. Willie was very keen on a telegram, or alternatively, silence. I told him, out of hand, that he was being far too hard on his poor parents, and that as we were getting married we had to patch up this feud; any form of bad feeling or argument made me feel physically ill. By early the next morning, as I lay with my joints locked rigid with cold, motionless on my damp mattress, watching the hoar-frost on the inside of the windows, I recognized Willie for the refugee he was. I wondered if it would make any difference to my warmth if I put my opened suitcase over the heavy grey army blankets that serviced my bed, in lieu of Willie, who was billeted two floors and three long corridors away from me.

The clock on the gothic mantelpiece in my room chimed at quarter-hour intervals through the night. I had known by my own watch, from early in the evening, that the clock was, as the Reverend Walsh would put it, lying. There was an increasing discrepancy between the real time and the one on its battered Victorian face. A different kind of mind from mine could have calculated at what points in the week the two would coincide. I was too preoccupied, however, even had I been capable of such mathematics, with listening to the chimes reverberating up the empty chimney stack with a ghastly resonance. The cold was actually far worse than the spooks that night. Willie had forewarned me about the singing chimneys – four distinct notes floating skywards like a heavenly chorus at unexpected moments of the night. And he had told me of a clanging, like the clanking of chains, which was in fact the nagging of the register-plate on the hall stove. He had even warned me about the various plumbing sounds and given a fair imitation of each one. I can still remember clearly how he described to me the winds coming unstopped from the Urals over the North Sea and directly into the Norfolk fens, hitting the British land mass across the Wash. This wind ignored King John's sunken treasure, coming directly to disturb the unpointed bricks of his father's rectory, the first house to make a stand against this Siberian invader.

Willie's father liked to give the impression of being a valiant but unsung pioneer. I don't know why 'unsung', since his life was dedicated to drumming his merits into the household. His wife, his geriatric gardener, and his congregation (all sixteen of them on Easter Sunday, Remembrance Day and Christmas morning, and just a regular seven on other days of worship) knew the tremendous sacrifices that he made daily for them. No one in the village, and I doubt even his wife, ever required him to rise at five and wash in cold water, but he did, for the good of his soul and the salvation of theirs. Just as no one required him to preach his sermons for as long as he did, in fact a Bolshie element in the guise of Mrs Peabody had actually dared to ask him not to. Nobody asked him, on the fringes of the Welfare State as they all were, to grow pumpkins in the heartless abundance which he did; or indeed for Mrs Walsh to make and give them the pumpkin jam that never set. The Vicar himself knew best, and Mrs Walsh felt obliged to keep up the semblance of village life even though her villagers had as good as forgotten what country life was like before *Coronation Street* and *Dallas* and bingo on Thursdays in King's Lynn. There was no television at the rectory, and Mrs Walsh thanked God, as she told me over dinner that night, that they had other things to amuse themselves with. I could see from the blank look on Willie's face that he had no notion of what these other things might be. I knew that he had a stash of Tin Tin books and a box of Swedish magazines hidden in the loft, which he had once smuggled up there years before but had never dared bring them down again, even to throw away. I wondered, though, what Mrs Walsh had hidden, and where.

There were mice in the skirting-boards at the rectory. The china pantry and the butler's pantry downstairs at the other end of the house gave an initial impression of being well stocked and quite available to mice. But on closer inspection I discovered that there were only Doomsday provisions of pumpkin jam and pumpkin chutney and damson chutney and fig chutney with their labels dating back to the years just after the war. Though the mice were hungry, they were obviously not that desperate. I had tried the jam at tea the day before, and it would take at least Doomsday to provoke a taste for it.

At a quarter to six, when the Reverend started to sing 'All Things Bright and Beautiful' in a menacing off-key baritone, I got up, and found Willie, and we left. I could see that he thought I was calling the whole thing off; and also that he wouldn't blame me for not wanting to associate with such arctic relations. All I wanted, though, was to get out and away; but not from him. I felt we were, if anything, closer, if that was all he had behind him. At least I had grown up in an atmosphere of well-meaning inanity, in a family that was stumbling thoughtlessly from one year to the next. There was nothing spiteful in my background. It was like an extra credit to him that he had turned out to be so well balanced and the nicest of men, having grown henpecked and sawboned from one cold night to the next.

So much for Willie's mother. My own mother wasn't like that at all. For a start I used to call her Mummy. When Willie came down to meet her I pre-arranged with her out of some sudden, and as it turned out quite unnecessary, embarrassment to call her by her Christian name – Vivienne. For someone as vague as Mummy was, this was not a good plan. Not only did she fail to remember William's name and relationship to me; she didn't answer to her own name once. I have rarely smiled mock-placidly as often as I did that afternoon. It was like a really bad press show. Five gin and tonics later I had also forgotten my name and what my relationship was to me and had gone to bed. Willie wandered around aimlessly and then went for a walk and bumped into my Uncle Jeremy in the garden. They went off to a pub together and Willie didn't seem to mind.

It has always seemed to me that a good way to choose where to travel is just to get an atlas and pick somewhere at random. To give a sense of purpose to the journey, it should be a place that one likes the name of, that is, the sound of the name or the shape it makes on the map. I've always liked travelling. When I was a child I used to dream of living in a house so big that I slept in a different room every night. William accused me of being more sexual than geographical in this whim; but it's really the sense of a new space that thrills me. I don't even care what that space is like when I get there, it is just the idea of it, the travelling, the opening of the door or the climbing of the stair.

The only thing that made having a base bearable was that I could keep my things there and go on buying more and more, and still find room to cram them in. Sometimes, though, I would get a kind of vertigo at seeing the same things in the same places day after day. Thank God the children grow and change. Once or twice at home I would look across a room as I went out and I'd think, if that side-table or that chair is still there when I get home I don't know what I'll do. I moved them.

25

Sestri Levante sounded nice on the map, I used to have a nursery toy called Piccolo Elefante – a not dissimilar name. It was Baia del Silenzio that did it though. Virtually everything I do or say or think comes from one side of me, and the other side is almost trepanned in its neglect. I always hold a part of me back, to keep it company, as it were. When I was a child I thought that I might be a saint, which would have accounted for my trials and made me happy. The element in me of self-sacrifice is matched only by that self-indulgence, but I grew to know the sacrifice first, the art of pleasing others. I discovered at an early age that I had a power over other people, I could make them do what I wanted, not always, but often.

Angelo and I had a good time together, I can't remember the details of it, but I know it was good. I still get a kind of glow thinking about it. I felt that I looked my best then. It doesn't matter what other people tell you, ultimately, you have to feel you look good yourself. You have to know it in your bloodstream. I can't remember when I started looking in mirrors, I suppose it was at some very early stage, judging by my own children who both became insufferably vain by the time they were a year old. I can remember, as a child, catching glimpses of myself as I walked down the long stairs at home and feeling a lovely calm sensation. It wasn't just that I was still there, had a reflection and so was alive, it was that I honestly liked what I saw.

I was twelve when I got my first absolute thrill at seeing myself. I had spent a miserable year at home, roaming through the garden under the unsubtly vigilant eye of Miss Hatherton, or 'Hathers' as I called my nanny-governess. Although nobody ever mentioned it, I was in the doghouse for the business with Uncle Bertie. The fact that he himself was in the hippopotamus house didn't make things any better. I felt that no matter what I did that year, it was wrong. I always need to be right, and seen to be in the right, it's the only way I can function. Without the general approval of friends and family, I seem unable to live my life. Then, I felt like an outcast.

Two days before Christmas Hathers took me to the pantomime for a treat. We always went to the pantomime for a treat at Christmas whether we wanted to or not. Hathers's mind was of the sort that could not grasp even the simplest plot or story-line. She found it hard to differentiate the characters or understand the ends of films and plays. However, we'd seen this particular production of *Dick Whittingon and His Wonderful Cat* for three years running. So, by the time our train pulled out of Dover station into the night, the bulk of the performance had been clearly explained, by me. Hathers was mulling over the implications of the bells. I sat staring into the dark space in front of me, which was a window on to the driver's cabin, lulled by the train and Hathers's sudden silence.

The more I looked into the blacked-out window, the more wonderful my darkened reflection looked to me. I became virtually hypnotised by my eyes and the outline of my hair against the inner curtain. I wanted everyone to look at me. The carriage was nearly empty, and Hathers was still totting up, I suppose, the chorus line. I turned to her, radiant with my new discovery. Hathers looked up absentmindedly but didn't seem to notice anything. I looked back, quickly, to make sure that the vision was still there; it was. Hathers still couldn't see it, but her powers of perception were notoriously limited.

In those days, of my pre-adolescence and pantomime-going, teenagers were either Mods or Rockers or they weren't really people at all. At the end of our compartment was a young Mod. His hair was cut so that it gave the appearance of being plastered down but it was actually clean and rebelliously – for a Mod – fluffy. He was a youth, I remember, with evident vanities of his own and I recall thinking that, on account of his distressingly bad complexion, he would be a subject likely to be overwhelmed by my beauty. Under the pretext of examining a toothpaste advertisement at his end of the compartment, I turned full face towards him. Quite preposterously, he looked away. For years after, I worried about what kind of future could lie in wait for a boy so impervious to feminine perfection. I turned away from him more in sorrow than in anger and hurried back to my seat to reassure myself that the loveliness was still there. It was: the boy was a confirmed fool. I sensed that somehow I would see myself through in life, and one day I would dazzle and shine.

Meanwhile, Hathers had got round to her annual stumbling block. 'How can bells talk, Ros?'

I didn't know then just how much bells could say, but I tried to explain the idea to her within the context of the play.

I was closer to Hathers than I was to anyone else. We were like partners, and I did everything that was in my power to conceal to the rest of the household her almost pathological lack of concentration and, frankly, wits. But even I find it hard to believe when I remember the inanity of our conversations in those days. As a governess, Hathers was useless. As a companion, she was a fine woman. It seemed to me, as a child, that Hathers should be designated the eighth wonder of the world. It was always a mystery how in the twentieth century a civilized Englishwoman could remain so sheltered from life. Her ignorance was somehow superhuman.

I didn't go to school, partly because Mummy could never quite get round to choosing which one I should go to, and partly because I was supposed to be dyslexic. I was about six years old when I realized that the day I became fully literate Hathers would have to go. We made uneventful progress through *Kitty and Rover,* but when we progressed to *Janet and John* I noticed that Hathers stumbled more often than I did, and I felt responsible for this. It had been my suggestion to liven up the test: 'This is Janet, this is John', and 'Where is Janet? Where is John?' by dividing it into two parts. I was Janet, and Hathers was John. Had I not so cast it, Hathers's illiteracy could have slipped by unnoticed possibly for years. As it was, I felt honour bound to conceal it with a more dramatic condition of my own.

My Uncle Jeremy, for some reason best known to himself, kept a pot of jasmine wedged in the conservatory with a pamphlet called *Dyslexia and Your Child.* I read this, committed the intelligible parts to memory and began to play my part as a handicapped pupil. From then on, nature walks, jigsaw puzzles and cinema matinées played the greater part in my education. We went to the cinema on Tuesday and Thursday afternoons, and spent most of the intervening times discussing details of the films. I used to think we were like Jewish scholars discussing the Talmud. We saw *Gone With the Wind* seven times, and after each one, as we emerged into the High Street still blinking from the dark to have our ritual toasted teacake and lemonade, Hathers asked, 'But what would have happened if none of them had met?'

Hathers and I used to get terribly emotional during these films

28

and weep profusely. I still do; in fact, the cinema is the only place where I can let myself go.

I love the sound of waves, that sort of tumbling swish that never ends. It makes me feel very insignificant, and I like that. It's restful. I get bored with myself sometimes. A whole life distils itself into a given number of seconds, but the waves go on for ever. For me, there was the moment when I knew that Hathers couldn't read, and the moment when Mummy and the others found me with Uncle Bertie. He'd been playing with me for months and it had never been wrong and then suddenly in that lone moment it became criminal. Then once there was a silly row on the telephone; and the first time I saw Angelo, and the time when I saw our dead baby at the Royal Free Hospital, a miniature perfect version of him cut in alabaster, and dead. And there was that one look of horror on Willie's face when I tactlessly offered to buy him a new tortoise. And there were other moments. Just a few others that go to make a life. It's more the silences than the things said. I can't let the waves down, and they can't let me down. They don't want to know my secrets, they don't try to scoop out my brain.

III

William

We used to go to South End Green because they sold nice cakes there and children flew kites on the Heath. It would be fair to say that chocolate and drifting were the two great passions of your life. Walking back from the beribboned hill to the tea-shop one afternoon down the steep incline of Tanza Road, your shoe strap broke, and you refused to go on. Gallant to a ludicrous degree (we are both five eleven, and you are arguably heavier than I am), I offered to carry you. You refused.

'I'll give you a piggy-back,' I said.

But even that failed to move you. You once said that a piggy-back was one of the nicest things in life, both giving one and taking.

'Well, wait here, and I'll get a taxi,' I told you, and I left you on the low stone wall of a house with a 'For Sale' sign on its gate. I made my way down to the rank, some five minutes away. I was back before ten minutes were up. You were sitting on the wall still, but beaming now and accompanied by a very effusive couple who seemed to know you so well you could have been related. We were vaguely house-hunting at the time. You were three months pregnant. You called out to me as I crossed the pavement.

'Now tell me the truth, Willie, do you like the house?'

I looked up at it for the first time and had a hazy impression of four storeys and a basement and a Victorian facade.

'Yes . . .' I said, a little uncertainly.

'Oh good,' you smiled, 'because I've just bought it.'

My jaw sagged, I suppose, further than you had ever seen it sag before.

'You don't have to look like that, we wouldn't buy it if you'd said you didn't like it.'

I was brought up in a world where divine retribution was meant to befall the unorthodox. Life had to run in certain channels, houses had to be bought through a due process involving surveyors and agents, solicitors and exchanged contracts. It seemed to me almost sacrilegious that a house should be bought, and sold, in under ten minutes, and by someone with a broken sandal, whom I had only recently married.

'What about the deeds?' I mouthed, lamely.

'We're going round to my solicitor's, now.'

'Rosalind, it is five o'clock on a Saturday afternoon.'

'Then we'll get him up off whatever lecherous sofa he is lying down on.'

The couple withdrew a little uneasily. It was clear that they looked on us as nutcases, and they didn't know which of us had the cash. We piled unceremoniously into my waiting taxi and headed across London to Knightsbridge. Half an hour later, with the dregs of my small talk rattling in my throat we arrived at Cadogan Square. You, the initiator of the scheme, had remained totally silent throughout the ride, leaving the vendors and me to make sociable noises. Nothing that the bearded, male half of that bespectacled couple had to say struck me as reassuring.

He had surmised, rightly, that I didn't want to go on hearing indefinitely about their Samantha's and Ben's progress at school, neither did I wish to hear about a new form of acupuncture that his wife was having. I hate needles. So, he stuck to the idiosyncrasies of the house, to the back door sticking on rainy days but just needing a good kick. He warned me about the stiffness of the upper sashes, and the harmless fungus growing in the airing cupboard . . . and that actually hardly any water came down the basement steps nowadays.

On our second turn round Cadogan Square, I remained as mute as you. The vendors cleared their respective throats, several times.

'It's jolly nice of you to pay the asking price,' the male vendor volunteered.

It occurred to me that I had no idea what this particular asking price was, so I asked you, in an undertone, 'How much?'

31

You smiled at me in a way you have, producing a kind of knee-capping effect. I was glad to be seated.

'Fifty thousand pounds.'

Of course the house was worth nearly a quarter of a million by the time we sold it. But then, at a time when I earned a tenth of its price in a year and thought myself lucky, it was more than I could bear. On the one hand I was appalled by the extravagance, on the other, I was disconcerted. One didn't move somewhere just because of nice chocolate cakes and kites. The taxi slowed down and I threw myself out of it, as a dramatic comment on our proposed move from the West End. I could hear behind me that the vendors were both concerned and impressed by this apparent kamikaze act. But I could see we were at the solicitor's, and I wanted to be the first out.

Ours was a nice house really. Right until the end. The back door still stuck in the rain but it always responded to a Pavlovian kick, and the upper windows were sealed for all the years we spent there. An inedible kind of chanterelle still spored its way out of the airing cupboard from time to time, but then the airing cupboard was not a place that could have borne a very close inspection of any kind. There were eleven rooms, two kitchens and three bathrooms, and every corner of every room was laden with bric-a-brac. This last was a mixture of the good, the bad and the ugly, with an emphasis on bargains.

At one point, living there in Tanza Road within the damp glory of our Hampstead mansion, there were you and I, Amadeo and the twins (Florence and Hattie), Candy, their nanny-cum-resident nymphomaniac, a cat, Mrs King, our daily housekeeper, and Fred, her protégé, who was my pet tortoise.

Later there was just you and me and Mrs King with her never-ending questions. I didn't dare sack her. There was too much she could have said, too many questions she could have raised with friends or neighbours. So I dried her out, as one might an alcoholic. Mrs King had been 'charring' as she called it, since she was four-teen. At a wizened sixty-three, she said that she felt more at ease with a duster in her hand than out of it. Bit by bit, I closed up the house, locking some rooms and barricading others. Then I began to rise earlier and earlier to tidy up and clean before she came. I don't think I have ever felt so mean. She had survived the war and the Blitz and her own widowhood, an almost invisible life of household drudgery. Yet, somehow, she had elevated her 'places' as she called them into a series of spotless kingdoms. She told me once that she loved working for us, because 'Her Nibs' – as she called Rosalind – was the untidiest person she had ever come across, and she got a 'genuine satisfaction' from setting things right.

Mrs King was born and raised in a steamy and begrimed backwater of South London to which in her eyes of exile north of the River Thames she remained steadfastly loyal.

'That was a decent bit of the world that was in my time,' she would say, sniffing nostalgically. 'Not that there's much left to judge it by nowadays . . . the ABC and the station . . . but you try getting a decent fishcake round that ABC. It can't be done. And who's in there with you?' Mrs King looked around her with narrowed eyes as though expecting the culprit to materialise there and then in our kitchen. 'A load of darkies,' she would pronounce almost triumphantly. 'They used to come round to the Baptist Church towards the end . . .'

The end was in 1953 when Mrs King's husband died of a stroke and a simultaneous and unconnected wave of West Indian and Asian immigrants settled along Balham High Road.

'Being a Christian, I don't mind them in church, and the Deacon could say some very moving things about them hot places and the Darkie Brigades in the war. But when it comes down to having my fishcakes and two slices handed across to me by a tarred hand and them standing in the bus queues and needing the chemist and for all I know sitting on the same public labatories, you just wonder, Mr Walsh, what Nelson fought for.'

This was a favourite phrase of Mrs King's, and it always led me to wonder what she thought the good admiral had fought for, and when, and against whom. It was never a topic that either of us pursued. Mrs King claimed that she had a 'nose' for foreigners. She was 'driven' to settle in the inhospitable neighbourhood of Belsize Park, fleeing their invasion of her own home territory. As a result, she seemed to bear a grudge that no amount of good-willed bantering could penetrate. She also waged her own campaign for the enforced repatriation of all but the true Balhamites, like herself.

Mrs King never rested in this campaign. Indeed it was she who alerted us to our own resident Rastafarian in the spring before you all trooped off to Larenguebec. I had, once or twice, passed this massive woolly-hatted West Indian on our stairs, as I imagine you must have done, and taken him to be a plumber or electrician working for us. For some reason, I had also failed to notice Candy's younger sister who has ensconced herself uninvited on the third floor, and apparently had been living there for weeks. This sister was sixteen, and a much podgier version of the nubile Candy herself. The girl had requisitioned a large room for herself and her Caribbean lover, and when asked to, nicely, refused to leave. She claimed that she had come to help out her sister, and that nothing would deflect her from this task. I pointed out in vain that we did not want two nannies, besides which she had not so much as lifted a finger since her arrival. The girl was unmovable. She told me that I was a bourgeois pig and that she would not be harassed into giving up her rights as an employee who could not and would not be pushed around. I reasoned gently with her, through a locked door, but all my entreaties were met with the same response. This was that the days when 'my sort' could push women around like slaves in the mines were over.

I appealed to Candy – who was, after all, her elder sister, and without whom we would not have had the problem in the first place – to do something about the situation. Miss Candy, however, through the hum of her supersonic hairdrier, said that, on principle, she never came between two people in a debate.

'But you're her sister, Candy,' I reminded her.

'Well, Mr Walsh . . .'

She always called me this, partly to tease me into some deeper familiarity, and partly to annoy me. I believe she knew that by that very 'Mr' I was further isolated in my otherwise entirely female household.

'Well, *Mr* Walsh, if you want to turn a young girl out on the streets, that's your business, but you can't really expect me to help you. Particularly,' she added, 'when all she's done is come and help us out here.'

After that, and for the next few weeks, my every query, appeal or suggestion was met by a defiant cry of 'racist' from the black man himself followed up by a threat to bring in the Race Relations Board and see what they had to say about it all.

Mrs King regarded the affair as the new beginning of the end and no less than she had expected, but not in this house, not here. During the siege, she kept Fred in a cardboard box under the stairs, and slipped him lettuce leaves in the dark. She stroked his horny shell and muttered soothingly, 'There, there, if they think they're going to eat you they've got another think coming.'

Eventually, it seemed that the virile Jamaican tired of Candy's sister and her revolutionary fervour, because the floorboards began to creak less and less often. Then, one evening, there was a great row, and weeping and the smashing of furniture – yours – yours – and the breaking of glass – possibly mine – and then there was a commotion on the stairs. The Rastafarian stormed out, followed by a weeping and suddenly vulnerable sixteen-year-old, and they never returned.

The room smelt of sweat and spent semen for a long time after that. Little butts of stale cigarettes kept coming out from under the rugs even after Mrs King had Hoovered and swept. And I found, in a glass-fronted bookcase, behind a spare set of *Chambers' Encyclopaedia,* a mouldy bowl of baked beans in a green sock. I have often wondered how long they could have lived there without our noticing if it hadn't been for Mrs King's prejudices. You told me that in Queen Victoria's time, a vagrant boy lived in Buckingham Palace, feeding on scraps, sleeping behind sofas and hiding in corridors, for a whole year before he was found.

I often felt like an alien in that house. You made Amadeo seem like a girl. Then you were all girls, like a voluptuous circus act, and you were the ring-master controlling it. They were all subtly in your power, even Candy, and the twins. You never asked for things, you just manipulated people into offering them to you. That is your art, or part of it. From the beginning you knew I didn't want him to have that name, Amadeo; it seemed unlucky.

I have never known how much you knew or recalled of his birth. There has been so much invention and denial. Way back, at the Royal Free Hospital, when Amadeo finally came, and failed to cry, you seemed locked in that moment. He just sighed and seemed to die. They took him out, and did all that is done to resuscitate a baby, but it was as though you thought he wasn't meant to live. He didn't even look new-born, with his grey clear water eyes staring up and the full head of pale curls and the chiselled mouth and that unearthly pallor of his skin. I've never seen a human child before or after so statuesque and calm.

The doctors told me first, calling me away from you. But in their haste to get the bad task over, they spilled the news tactlessly, searching for words and then just blurting out, 'It's touch and go . . . You'd better warn your wife.'

At the point when the baby sighed, on the slab at the end of your trolley, I had this funny feeling that it was about to talk. I know it's absurd. Then, when the doctors stood there, hovering in a kind of knot, I couldn't sort my thoughts into coherence, but I was thinking of that when I asked them, 'What did it say?'

'It was . . . almost a stillbirth, Mr Walsh,' one of the doctors added wistfully. And I remember thinking that the staff would have preferred to have been able to put a clear note in the day's log-book, '15.45 hrs. Still born boy, 9lb. 3 oz.', and close the entry effortlessly.

There was a long silence then, broken by, 'I'll have to be getting along.'

I went back to you, Rosalind. You were lying crumpled and swollen, exhausted on your trolley bed. I sat with you for a while, holding your hand, and stroking your tangled hair. Then I told you, that the baby was alive, but still delicate. You interrupted me right from the start, just saying no and no and no. It's been no at times ever since. There was no new baby, no alabaster son, just your own burden of guilt buried in a tiny coffin at a funeral that you invented, in an imaginary grave that you hid from me for years. Even later, when Amadeo pulled through and was home, you insisted that there had been twins. Identical boy twins, and one had died for you.

The nurse came to you, and a Catholic priest to comfort you in your tiredness, but you sent them away. I saw the baby again, that same evening, in the intensive care unit. You refused to, but I needed to, even though most of all I wanted him to come alive for you. It was strange, wasn't it, to see that stilled vision of Angelo staring up at us from the end of your bed? It was in intensive care that they first asked for a name. The baby had a tag on his wrist and on his cot, just saying 'Baby Walsh' and then a number. It was the Scottish attendant who asked me, 'Will you be giving it a name?'

Everyone saw our child as an 'it', and the more I heard that reduction to anonymity of a human life, the more I wanted to give him a name of his own.

So I went back to you, down the long corridors and the network of lifts, breathing in the wax polish from the floors. The pale walls seeming to cave in on me. You had cut off, though, and were refusing to recognize that you had had a child at all. You were still Rosalind Palliser, the actress, who was sleepy now and couldn't be disturbed, not even by me. For you, the family was in no danger. In your mind your son was dead, stillborn, destroyed by you, and you dealt with this supposed failure by withdrawing and pretending. I was there, and you were there, and Jimmy could be called up to make you laugh if needed, so why the fuss? An Italian nurse came back with a hot drink for you. I could see you resented her presence for trying to pin you down to the reality of a room in a ward, to a hospital that you were already wiping out of your memory, to an event that was being erased from your life.

I appealed to her, privately. And she returned, as unwelcome as before, and asked you, on your own, what you wanted to call your son. We hadn't fixed on any names, you see. We thought that each child should get a name at birth to suit his or her personality. I heard only the end of your reluctant discussion.

'. . . is still your baby, is alive, not dead,' the nurse told you in her broken English.

'No.'

'You must care enough to give it a name.'

'No,' you insisted and turned away.

The nurse was shocked, almost frightened. She shared your Catholicism, but carried her own Mediterranean blood, rooted in childbirth and the rearing of children that made them sacred, all children, anybody's, yours and mine.

She came out, shaking her head sadly.

'Is no good. You make him a name for now.'

My mind went blank and I couldn't. 'I want an Italian name,' was all I could say.

'Is no true, she no love him, eh?' the nurse appealed to me, as though to reaffirm her faith in human nature. I held her back from you this time, though; we were only struggling for a name. You had struggled to give birth that day and gone through more than she or I could ever understand. So who were we to criticize whatever measure you took to defend yourself against the day's events?

'Then call him Amadeo,' the nurse said firmly, 'loved by God.'

'No,' I said, and left her, little knowing that you would later say yes. Names have their own power, Rosalind, and that one didn't seem right.

IV

William

Falling in love is a terrible thing, Rosalind, perhaps the only thing that breaks all other ties. There is nothing that I wouldn't do for you. Nothing I want to change in you, despite all your maddening faults. It is as though the faults help to make up the person that I love. So when I say, you did this, and you did that, that's all I'm saying; I'm not accusing you. I don't blame you for anything. I've never really fathomed what you feel about Amadeo, but I know that you did your best and I wouldn't ask for more than that.

When I went to visit you with our twin girls, two weeks after Amadeo was born, you were in a ward with three other women, each with your baby in a plastic crib at the foot of your metal bed. It was a Thursday afternoon, and I remember that I arrived late. I had left home early, but the twins were, as ever, unmanageable without you. They have their own names, but not their own faces, and they tease me enough without my trying to identify them separately. What perverse plasma runs through their veins to make them so unapproachable? Even when they were babies, they had more caprice in their eyes than you or I have in our whole bodies. Notice that I don't call it malice. It's just another image, a mask, and underneath it there are two gifted children struggling under a pre-cociousness that frightens me, as I think it frightens them.

They were six then, and they had just started talking in public. Although I never caught them at it, I still believe that they talked to themselves, unobserved, years, before they made this début. Until their recent decision to speak, they had been supposed to be autistic. Everyone, except you, said they were. You wouldn't hear of it though; you used to laugh and say, 'They're just sweeties, just pretending. Don't worry about it.'

In one week we passed from having two identical silent dunderheads whom neighbours pitied, to having a pair of child prodigies. It was only a five-minute walk to the hospital but it took us all afternoon to get there. It must be a fine line, where a practical joke becomes delinquency, and where delinquency becomes crime. Our twins began their lives as infant delinquents, progressed rapidly to the criminal and have now in their thirteenth year tamed themselves into mere jokers. Tamed themselves, mind, because nothing that I or Candy or Mrs King or any of their teachers have ever said seems to have made the slightest impression on their outrageous behaviour. I do belive, though, that the calmness of your example has guided them in some mysterious feminine way. They fell on the outer edges of the field of your power.

That day, one of them feigned a convulsion outside the Half Moon pub, while the other wept crocodile tears on the kerb. Then both of them crawled through the bent railings of the railway embankment and ran across the tracks, causing the signalman to chase after them, apoplectic with rage. It was by no means the first time that they had done this. The year before, the railway authorities had actually traced them back to our address and turned up with a policeman. The sight of our two girls in their starched pinafores, with their hair plaited immaculately and their pouting smiles, seemed to soften him. The two of them sitting mutely on matching chairs in the quiet drawing-room staring sadly at their nursery books was too much for the officer. When he questioned our angelic five-year-olds, they said nothing (it was before the days of their speech). But they turned on him such pathetic and appealing faces, each with a matching tear of maligned innocence forming in her right eye, that the police officer became quite emotional. All this, combined with the tremendously professional speech on your part about the silent horrors of autism, with a heart-rending description of the suffering that you and the two cherubs went through from day to day, was almost more than I could stand. The policeman was virtually bowing with apologies by the time he reached the hall. Had he glanced back into the drawing-room, he would have seen the twins bent double in silent glee.

From that time on, they took full advantage of the signalman's impotence. He didn't dare go back to the police and accuse 'little babies'. He himself had been accused of hallucinatory drunkenness, and the twins knew it. They threw empty beer bottles into his signal-box, they piled up all the wine and whisky bottles retrieved from the dustbins of Tanza Road. They ran across the tracks, zig-zagging over the electric lines, flaunting his ineptness at catching them and risking the vicious current.

Any kind of interference in their pranks had been met in the old days with daylong fits of rocking. Then, later, it was met by bursts of hysterical screaming. The twins screamed in chorus, and at a pitch that was so distressing I couldn't bear it. So I learnt to wait patiently until the girls were ready to come back to me, and to appreciate the rare quiet moments when I had two stunning young ladies beside me. When they were babies, I used to cuddle them. But as soon as they were strong enough to resist, they did. Only Amadeo liked his cuddles, and stories and walks. After the miserable coldness of my own childhood, I really wanted to make a child happy. If trying was all that was needed perhaps the twins would have been more normal too. Now, at least, they seemed happy with their pranks and deceits.

On Thursday mornings, a registrar went round the Royal Free Hospital Maternity Ward, registering the babies' names, to save their busy parents the trouble of going to the Registry Office. Thus Amadeo Walsh, our son, was named in my absence, by you, with the name thought up by the Italian nurse. I think for you it was like a legal insistence on his death, he was an angel, not real. By the time I arrived with the girls, the birth certificate was signed and stamped and five hours old. I suppose I felt that it didn't give him the right start in life. I asked, 'Why?'

'It's a lovely name,' you told me, 'it means beloved of God.'

I remembered the Italian nurse and her grief, and a bad feeling sank into me that I wouldn't be adequate to protect this child from the world. It seemed, by some magic, that I could keep you, and even the twins, safe but by naming our son with that mournful name you had set him outside my meagre power. Things happen, and are dealt with. Usually, I deal with them. It is I who gather up the dead sparrows on the sideboard, and the tins of crushed snails that the twins keep under their beds. And I deal with Candy's sporadic weeping fits, and Mrs King's occasional explosions. As your agent would say, in his incongruously prim voice, when another dollop of shit hits the fan, I duck, and when the fan shorts, I unplug it. Somehow, though, the sight of the birth certificate with its red italics, and that Italian name beside my own was too much for me, and I wept.

Even as my face crumpled, I knew I was being a drip, and I was acutely aware of the other three women in their beds, with the plastic cribs latched on to the railings at their feet, all pretending to look away. I tried to draw strength from your touching my hair, knowing that within seconds you would fade out of the set and cut off, until long after I'd pulled myself together. I also noticed, perhaps for the only time, ever, that I was embarrassing the twins. I buried my face in the green hospital counterpane and thought desperately how I could raise it again with any semblance of control. Then Jimmy came to my aid, as he so often came to yours. Still muffled by the bedclothes he explained, in his heavy Italo-English,

'It is alla too much for me. The boys, my friends, they noa tell me it is a, how you say, emotional like this, lika the football.' You all smiled, relieved.

'Did you know that Heliogabalus died head-first down a latrine?' you asked us.

'Yes, I replied, truthfully, and then regretted it as you gave a sad shrug.

'I didn't really,' I lied.

You smiled and looked up, suddenly radiant. Then we left.

You were always full of 'did you knows'. I suppose you still are, except that it's harder to find such a wealth of accumulated eccentricities as you had amassed before we met. Over the years, you almost exhausted your stock, and have had to recycle some of your favourites.

So you had your did you knows, and I had my impersonations and my comic walk. That same night, of the naming day, I went to Highgate cemetery. I had often been there before. I found it hard to pass the massive gateways and the rusting railings without going in sometimes and paying homage to all those austere graves, so reminiscent of my home and the graveyard by my father's church.

When the children refused to speak, and when they rocked, moving in perfect unison with one another but so utterly out of phase with the world, I visited those graves. And when you sat and stared into the back garden, staring and scanning as though out to sea, I went. I knew on those days that there were real waves outside for you, salt water lapped at our back door, and even the sounds of the tumbling from the drier were converted into beach sounds. I couldn't reach you on those days. We would make love for hours on end: but your absence invented my own, and I felt myself dragged as by a tide out into the nothingness you lived in.

On those days, I would go down to South End Green, to the *pâtisserie*, and buy a chocolate gâteau, and you would smile, as near to ecstasy as you ever came. It was like feeding delicacies to a caged bird, or tending some volatile hot-house flower.

When I went to the cemetery, after seeing you in hospital, it was late September, and the brambles were going wild. All along the outer railings, massive suckers had stretched out across the more untended graves. Some of the berries were ripe and pouting through the prickly leaves. I never ate the berries there. I don't suppose many people did. They were almost unnaturally luscious and tempting as one passed, losing the way from time to time in the overground warren of measured stones and plots. Sometimes, distracted by the birds and trees and the hush that filled the place, interrupted only by the occasional passing car outside, my hand would pick a fruit, and then drop it, almost disgusted by the act, remembering where that lush fertility came from.

I had decided that our own Amadeo Walsh, who had sighed and died but been resuscitated, and given a ghostly name, could be prejudiced by my morbid nostalgia, and I resolved to stop traipsing through the bracken and the gathering weeds. From now on, with our new son already two weeks old and waiting to be brought home, I had to stop nourishing my melancholia and let the brambles run their natural course. You kept saying that your baby was dead, stillborn. Now I had to change your mind; show you his moving hands, make you hold and accept him. You had given birth to him, been in labour for seven hours sweating and moaning in the labour ward. They had been your contractions, it was your pain. Whatever pain I felt, I had felt by proxy. The dark shadows that gathered like new bruises under your eyes. All that you knew of his living was that one sigh, having carried him for nine months in your womb. Who was I to criticize your momentary grief? It was imaginary to some, but it was real to you. You seemed locked in the moment of this apparent expiry. Even after you accepted Amadeo, you did so as a twin, an identical twin whose brother died at birth in the Royal Free Hospital. Thus the Amadeos were born in your mind. I tried to understand and help you.

Perhaps my first effort was to forgo my visit to Highgate, even though I had a natural affinity with cemeteries. I had grown up beside one, played in it as a child, and hidden there for refuge from the incessant nagging of my home. There was the rectory, and between it and the church, there was a graveyard. It was at once our no man's land and all that divided us from God.

You and I kept a lot of secrets from each other, or, rather, we still keep them. Some people are very open with their lives, and others hide things away. We are both, I would say, of the latter sort. I don't know which of us is worse, or more extreme about it. You keep secrets from yourself, but I suppose we all do, it's just that you keep more unorthodox ones than other people. I used to hide things at home, not just my Tin Tin books – anything. It gave me an inner happiness to know that there were little things that couldn't be touched by my parents' severity, simply because they didn't know about them. I learnt to tell lies very young; they were what you call white lies. Often they stopped other people's feelings from being hurt; usually, they protected my own. Only naturally devious people can understand each other in this way. Outsiders are shocked or worried by the habit. I honestly think it's a good one, and should be adopted, if anything, more widely.

At school, I became expert at the art of lying, perfecting it almost to my present-day standard. Apart from a weekend in Amsterdam some years ago, and a couple of months' flirtation with a singer from Notting Hill, there has been nothing kept from you that could have done you any harm. I don't believe that those infidelities really did you any harm either, but, had you known, they might have hurt your pride. I am not mathematician enough to calculate the extent of your sexual infidelities to me. I know, though, that you are not one to be done by as you did. I also believe that the term infidelity in your case is not appropriate. I believe that something in you always stays faithful to me. Maybe I am lying to myself now, but what harm does it do?

I have told so many lies since you and the twins came back from Larenguebec that some days it has felt as though I were wrapped in cobwebs. There comes a point when it's hard work remembering who has been told what and when. One of the good things about Sestri Levante is that nobody asks us about the children. There are no head counts, no evasions.

V

Rosalind

I think William is obsessed by numbers. I knew an actor once who computed the whole of world history in units of four. He had spent years multiplying and dividing all the famous dates. One was hardly going to spend a corresponding length of time checking them, so I suspect it was only all the dates that were divisible by his magic number. What did it prove? I don't know, and I don't think he did, other than that he'd had a lot of time to spare and a hang up on mental arithmetic. He told me, when I was unromantic enough to ask, that he did it just for the wonder of the thing. William's trouble is the two-eyed monster, the two-headed beast, the double-sided knife, the two-faced lady, and, no doubt, the twins.

Whenever he gets serious, which is more often nowadays than he used to, he goes on about Amadeo. He calls him 'the Amadeos' as though he were a mountain range and not a little baby. I have always been accused of having a sick sense of humour, and I confess that it is a little extreme, maybe even perverse. William, though, seems more to have momentary lapses of tact. Frankly, a woman doesn't want to be reminded of a stillborn baby. Willie and I have never actually discussed the uncanny resemblance to Angelo that the child had. I only saw it once, and I couldn't bear it. It was the most unreal thing I have ever seen. I couldn't talk about it for years. It was when I got back from Larenguebec, I seemed to miss that immaculate five-minute life. I wish now that I hadn't been so rash as to mention it to William, though. He's usually so good about everything, and understanding.

I must have scratched his record bringing up the still birth, because he can't seem to forget it now. Two years after I mentioned it, with the sea all around us, and nothing to do but lie back and relax, what does Willie keep coming up with?

'What *do* you feel about the Amadeos?'

I probably don't really mind. I keep going back to things myself. It's the labelling that I don't like. I feel that he's obsessed by twos because he's convinced I'm schizophrenic, and I don't like being put in a specimen jar like that. Why does he think I'm mentally ill? Because when we were blissfully happy on our honeymoon, I met the most wonderful man in the world and I fell in love with him too. Why did I fall for Angelo? Because there was something mysterious and unique about him. Why was this? I don't know. Willie says, because there are two of me in here, one that needs stability, one that needs change. Maybe there are, maybe there are two people inside every woman, or more. Who hasn't given herself, in deed or thought, to two men at once? Or, rather, by turns; but often with no more than minutes between each turn. Who hasn't watched a film and imagined herself kissing the star and then turned and kissed her lover? How can I explain all this to him? He doesn't understand, couldn't, has to evaluate everything in terms of himself. If I sleep with someone else, then he has failed me. It isn't like that. Angelo had nothing to do with William. I just happened to be honeymooning at the time. When I think about it, though, it was unfortunate timing. To think of all the days when I've stared out to sea and willed some lovely creature to come out and please me! Instead, it happens on Day One of a happy marriage.

Hathers used to say that thinking was very bad for the brain. It could be that this was her greatest discovery. I wish she had followed it up with a foolproof antidote for when the thoughts have set themselves in motion, and they won't stop. But then, Hathers never could grasp more than one idea at a time. I'm quite content to remember each and every moment of my six weeks in Sestri Levante, until I consider what other people would think of me if they knew. I don't like to think about what Willie would feel either. It just didn't have anything to do with him. It was a wonderful honeymoon. It is so often outsiders who come in and spoil things. I never judge people on surface values: there's always so much more to see if it gets even half a chance to show itself. So I never look at people and decide about them out of hand – unless, of course, they're ugly or boring.

Lots of people thought Hathers was boring, but she wasn't at all. The worst she could get was a little bit tedious when she asked the same questions too many times. I liked it, though, the way she saw things through a completely different lens to me. I would never have thought of half the things I used to if it hadn't been for her funny questions. I always wanted to do things right, and for people to be astounded by it.

Mummy always used to say that I was a good girl, whatever I did. You see, she was too vague to notice what I was doing, and, of course, too busy. She used to entertain a lot. I inherited my vagueness from her. Hathers was short-sighted, and she used to wear glasses. She told me that she'd had perfect eyesight until she was eleven; but then she'd caught measles. When she'd got better, she was left in a myopic haze for ever. She said that I used to be different, before I was eleven, and then I got vague. But I didn't ever have measles, even German measles. Even when I was very young, I used to think about being good. Hathers never told on me, and I thought that made me responsible in a way. So if I did something naughty, and I could tell Mummy without getting Hathers into trouble, I used to go to look for her and confess. It was as though she'd already made up her mind that I was her good girl, and she didn't want to be bothered with anything that spoiled that image for her. Then I'd regret having talked and bothered her, and regret having spoilt something for myself too. It made me feel comfortable to be good, to know that everyone approved.

I used to be very clean. I've always liked having baths; deep hot baths with salts and big towels. I can remember that I used to really scrub myself. It was a purifying ritual. Sometimes I wished I could go to school, any school, to meet other children and find out if I was learning the right things. It never became a major issue at home, though, and it kept Hathers safe in her job. I worked it out that after she had seen me through my school years, no one would have the heart to turn her out. I used to worry a lot about her future. She came to us when I was three, and I don't think she could have easily managed any other employment. She made my nursery very special for me. We used to eat a lot of toasted tea-cakes and Toblerones, and chocolate cakes that she would cut before they were properly cooked. We had a book called *Fanny Farmer's Boston Cook Book* that had the most wonderful chocolate cake in it. Even Mrs King could make that one.

So Hathers and I had our nature walks and our jigsaws, the cinema and our sticky teas, and nothing ever seemed to go wrong until the day that they found me with Uncle Bertie. The funny thing was that Uncle Bertie had been coming to see me for years, and everybody liked him. I liked him too, but at first I didn't really like playing with him. He was rumbustious the way jolly uncles are in films, but I didn't like kissing people and playing cuddling games. Nobody else ever tried to; even Mummy knew that I didn't like to be hugged. Uncle Bertie actually used to get quite shocked, and he used to say to Mummy, in front of me, whenever he got the chance, 'That girl of yours has got no manners, Vivienne!'

It always upset her when anyone criticized me; not that they often did. It made her face go all disappointed under her foundation. Once or twice she said to me, after Uncle Bertie had gone, 'Do be nice to Bertie.'

I thought it was Uncle Bertie who didn't like me, because I did try to be nice; I played games with him and let him come on our nature walks and we'd go out to tea together, and to the swings, and even when he pushed me much too high, I didn't cry or protest. After his visits were over, though, we kept on having these little pep talks, when Mummy would say things like, 'I'm sure you didn't mean to, darling, but Bertie is feeling a bit sensitive and I think you may have upset him.'

I asked Hathers to come with us when we went out, but she didn't seem to understand that I needed her. You see, I never had needed her before, and I'd begun to spend quite a bit of time on my own, reading mostly. She used to call that her dreamy time, because she would sit by the fire and stare into the flames and daydream and think up a whole string of film questions to ask me later. I even asked Mummy to come sometimes, but she'd say, 'Now that you're eight, darling, I think you really ought to try.'

I tried everything I could think of, but I didn't know what Mummy wanted me to do. Could it really matter how many times I kissed my Uncle Bertie, and for how long I sat reluctantly in his lap?

At first I tried to hide from him that I didn't like being too close. Then, when he kept on coming, more and more often, and telling tales on me, it got so that I was only just civil to him. I knew I was in the wrong, everybody told me so, but I couldn't help it.

There was a beech wood at the end of the garden, and then a paddock, and a little shed between the two, and next to the shed there was my swing. I had almost stopped using the swing, since whenever Uncle Bertie was around he would push me too hard and I didn't like heights. If I didn't use it when he wasn't there, then I could truthfully say that I didn't use it any more. I didn't usually mind telling lies, but since everyone was so cross with me about him, I thought it better to be 'catechism straight'.

It had been raining, I remember, and the grass was long and wet. I had on my Wellingtons and a skirt that Hathers was very fond of but I secretly hated. It was August, and Uncle Bertie and I were looking for mushrooms. As usual, I hadn't wanted to go with him, and I could see that he was still annoyed with me. When we got to the clearing and the swing, he said, 'I'll give you a push, and we'll make it up.'

He had a really nice face, handsome and blond with very sparkling eyes and a moustache. I suppose he was about thirty-eight or so. He was my mother's stepbrother. I think he was in business. That afternoon, though, his face was tense and strange looking, and I didn't trust him. I don't know what had happened back at the house that morning, but he was very cross. He tried to grab me, to force me on to the wet swing. I ran round, quicker than he did, and pulled the swing away. Then I pushed it back to him, and it hit him hard in the chest.

He was furious. I had never done anything like that before, and I didn't know what would happen, I just stood and stared at him expecting the ground to open up and drag me down into hell. Instead, Uncle Bertie leapt at me and dragged me to the swing. Then he sat down, with me, still cataleptic with fear, and he spanked me. I had never been hit before. Not a slap or a punch even from another child. I had scarcely been touched even in kindness. I had been untouchable, and now suddenly he was hitting me hard, under my skirt, and the wet grass rocked with the swing and the cloth covered my face and I didn't know how I could ever live again. He must have hit me very hard, because I hurt for days afterwards and there were bruises too. When he stopped, I couldn't move. I wanted to run away, but I couldn't move. I was making a funny noise, like a strangled sob.

'We'd better hide,' he said, 'before you get into worse trouble.'

Then he took me into the little shed, and held me very tight and stroked my hair and spoke kindly to me. I kept wondering how Mummy would feel if she knew how bad I'd been after all the times she had asked me to be nice. And I was frightened for Hathers, who could never have controlled me if I had been bad; and there I was huddled in the wood shed, chastised like in the Bible. We stayed there for what seemed ages, hugged together, and Uncle Bertie said it was all right, and we were friends now, and that sometimes people had to fight to become real friends. I remember feeling very grateful to him because he wasn't going to tell, and because he hadn't hurt me more, and because I was able to relax in the dark with him and not feel responsible for everyone.

After that, he visited me just as often, but we were friends and used to go for walks together and do my jigsaws and 'hide' in the wood shed, and talk quietly. Apart from Hathers, he was the only person to take any real notice of me and he was very kind. He used to help me with my catechism and bring me books – I owned up to not being dyslexic and he promised not to tell – and he used to tell me stories of when he was a prospector in Australia and about the Aborigines. And I was back in the Angel House, as we used to call it whenever anyone was specially good.

The summer came, and we went swimming together several times, and had a lot of fun and some lovely picnics. One day, though, we had another row. It was a cold day, and I'd stayed in the river too long. My teeth were chattering when I got out and I was fumbling for my vest. Uncle Bertie offered to help me get dressed, and I refused. Then he said, 'Come on, you're not shy with your own uncle are you?'

I don't know why I said what I did, it just came out. I said, 'You're not my uncle!'

I couldn't read the look on his face; it was so complex. In that flash second that he let his feelings show, he was both hurt and angry, along with all the other things he felt. His voice sounded very formal when he spoke.

'Come here.'

I thought he was going to hit me again, but I knew I deserved it because Mummy had told me never to mention that I knew.

Instead, he dried me all over, and then kissed me in lots of different places that I didn't like. He kissed me lots and lots of times, and in between he would look me in the eyes and say, 'So, are you still ashamed of me?'

I didn't want him to touch me without my clothes on, and I was very cold, shivering, and I was ashamed of myself. Then he dressed me and held me tight, and it was a bit like it used to be before, and he told me over and over again, 'I am your family.'

When I got home, I washed off all his kisses and scrubbed myself with the loofah and the pumice stone. That night, when Mummy came to kiss me goodnight, she pecked my forehead as she always did and she said, 'Bertie seemed so upset about something at dinner tonight, *do* be nice to him darling. It's so sweet when you are.' Then I knew that it was like celery and tapioca, something that I had to get used to, and pretend to like.

So the months went by, all through my ninth and tenth years, and Uncle Bertie came and sought me out, and took me to the wood in the summer, and to the wood shed in winter. When I think how much I like the new and the unexpected now, it surprises me to remember how little I liked them as a child. Hathers and I always sat in the middle of the same row towards the back of the cinema, and we had 'our' table in the tea-shop, and certain fixed routes through the gardens and grounds. Whenever anything new was tried in the wood shed, I didn't like it. I knew, though, that Uncle Bertie would always be gentle as long as I didn't cry or complain.

People say of childhood memories that everything gets physically bigger with the passing of time. But Uncle Bertie was an exception. I have often listened with interest to girls remembering the first time they saw an erect penis. I hear of a mixture of feelings – fear, lust, surprise, astonishment, disgust. I was shocked when my uncle first opened his trousers, because it seemed that this was something that should only be done in the lavatory. It was actually some weeks before I noticed that he had anything untoward inside them.

Despite all that happened over those two and a half years, I remained, technically, a virgin.

It was just before my tenth birthday that we went the whole way, even though this whole way left me virgo intacta. I was preparing for my first communion at the time, and I was obsessed by the idea of being pure. Our constant 'hiding' worried me immensely; secrets, I felt, were one thing, but actually hiding had to be bad. I tackled my uncle with these doubts one day, and he gave me a lecture on growing up and the true nature of sin. He told me, in effect, that certain things had to be done, but must never be talked about to other people. Then he explained to me about having babies and periods and a number of other things that I had had some hazy knowledge of but no clear idea. He was very insistent about puberty and the segregation of the sexes in adolescence. I listened, fascinated, but not entirely believing him as he told me lurid tales of wedding nights and teenage pregnancies. He claimed that there was virtually a worldwide conspiracy to suppress any talk of sex with little girls, whose only hope of initiation was by the enlightened such as he. Ever since the beginning of our hiding times, Uncle Bertie had bound me to silence and total fidelity. He must have lived in a world where every other male was a potential child molester, because he warned me to steer clear of everyone from my Uncle Jeremy to the usher at the cinema.

That day there was no fumbling in the dark, instead, I pleaded a sore throat, went to bed early, and pondered the implications of his words. The sin, it would seem, was not in the doing, but in the telling. Despite these reassurances, I felt that I must have a second opinion. I was going to my communion classes three times a week, or rather once a week, as on the other days Father Ingot came to me. Father Ingot had a way of staring at people that was so intense it produced a kind of physical uneasiness. One of his favourite sentences was 'I suffer for you, child', accompanied by a searching and truly agonized stare. Early on in our communion proceedings Father Ingot had made it clear that the purification of our souls was all that he lived for. Since twice a week he came exclusively to me, I came to believe myself responsible for the alleviation of his not inconsiderable pain. He had intimated, on several occasions, that a confession – unofficial – of any misdemeanours would go a long way towards easing this suffering.

Over the months of his preparatory classes, I thought up all the peccadilloes that I had committed over the past several years, and duly confessed them. He seemed not only unimpressed, but disappointed. I used to lie awake at night, listening to the gentle snoring of Hathers in the next room, wondering what I could do to de-activate his holy stare. I invented a number of minor sins and confessed to these. Again, Father Ingot seemed to be angling for some more specific, incomprehensible admission. I realize now, with hindsight, that he wished to know if I touched myself. At the time, though, I was mystified by his veiled hints, his stares and his wounded glances.

Something of his zeal did manage to permeate through to me, however, because it was on account of his thrice-weekly diatribe that I had challenged my uncle. After our tête-à tête about the facts of life, I decided to check on some of the things he'd told me. I started with Hathers, who was very reluctant even to approach the subject. I pointed out to her that I was now ten years old and had no one but her to instruct me. I argued that although I could get through life without any formal education (and could even have managed as an illiterate), if it was true that I was going to have one of these 'periods', then I should know about it. Hathers was very flustered.

'Where have you been getting all these ideas?' she asked me, suddenly jealous, it seemed, that I might have been secretly to the cinema without her and accidentally seen 'one of those Swedish films', as she called them. I promised her that I had merely overheard some idle chat from the other children at communion class, and wished to hear from her own lips if what I had heard was true. Hathers cleared her throat.

'Did you say it was tea time, Ros, dear?'

'It's half-past nine,' I reminded her gently. Hathers ran her fingers absently through her grizzled hair and shifted uncomfortably in her chair.

'Then sit down and you can explain about *Duck Soup* again – there's a lot there we still need to understand.' Hathers very sweetly always included me in her waves of noncomprehension. Some five weeks before, we had taken a bus into our local town and seen, for our ritual Thursday matinée, the Marx Brothers in *Duck Soup*. The effect on my nursery companion had been nearly fatal. We had sat up for the best part of the night trying to reduce the stream of zany gags to a simple order that could be catalogued and stored in Hathers's brain, somewhere between 'C' for *Casablanca* and 'E' for *East of Eden*. We had then gone back, day after day, and sat through the film again. It was to no avail, though, because the more we saw of Harpo's and Groucho's antics the more bewildered she became. For over a fortnight, her waves of anxiety threatened to become tidal and engulf us both in a kind of nervous collapse. Then her waves of anxiety subsided to mere flurries and a number of extra sessions, like the one Hathers was proposing to me.

I said, 'You know what it's like to worry about things that you don't understand; well now I need to know about growing up and bleeding.'

I reckoned that she would hardly refuse such a kindred call after all the time that she herself had spent in a nebulous and unexplained state of darkness. Then she blushed a slow blotchy crimson, stared down at her ugly 'sensible' shoes and began to talk.

'This is all most unfortunate, I don't know how you haven't understood, I went to such a lot of trouble to explain it all last year, or the year before, don't you remember, Rosalind, about the horses?'

I vaguely recalled an earlier conversation, when Hathers had stumbled through a most unlikely tale about the horses at the end of the wood falling in love and getting married and then having piggy-backs and babies. At the time, I had felt extra worried about Hathers for a few days, fetching her hot-water bottles to hold during the day and extra cups of tea. She had blushed terribly at the time of the horses and the story had seemed to touch her somewhere in a way that quite escaped me. Looking back later, I recalled her earlier plea. 'You do understand what I'm saying, don't you, Ros?' she had begged, with such contortions of her hands and face that I felt alarmed for her sanity. 'Of course I do,' I'd lied, trying to calm her as best I could.

'Do you promise me, promise me that you understand?'

So I promised, not knowing what I promised other than my good intentions to her own urgent fantasies. If Hathers needed to believe that horses gave each other piggy-backs around the field, and cavorted down to the village church in white lace veils to say their catechism and their creed, I would promise her it was so, if it made her feel easy.

Then, two years later, the tears came to her eyes and she blamed herself for what she saw as yet another proof of her failure.

'Surely you remember the horses, dear?'

I suppose it was true, at least for her. She had tried to bring me up more liberally than she had been herself. She had overcome her own myriad inhibitions and explained in her advanced spinsterhood about the birds and the bees to an eight-year-old who had no idea what she was talking about and so had lost the privilege of an early sexual education. Or, rather, had slipped unwarned into a world of abuse; the condoned abuse of a restless uncle. When Hathers talked about the horses that time, she had laid a lot of stress on marriage. Piggy-backs were only all right after marriage.

It never occurred to me, at the time, that she wanted her tale to apply to human beings too, and more specifically to me. Just as, I suppose, it never occurred to her in her myopic innocence to check the sexes of the horses in our field. They were, in fact, both mares, and the only possibility of Hathers's scenario coming true would have been by an equine equivalent of the virgin birth, or, less exotically, by artificial insemination. I hadn't the heart to tell her this. Under all her embarrassment, I could see that she was proud of being able to relay a fact that she had observed herself. At some point in her earlier career – and whatever that was, I never knew – Hathers must have seen with her own eyes the astonishing sight of a sexually aroused stallion; and, for once, she had followed a plot unaided.

'What about the periods though?' I asked.

Sanitary towels were discussed and then a probable age for my beginning to need them. After this we never discussed them, or sex, again, not ever. Even when I was discovered under my uncle, Hathers managed to pretend it hadn't happened.

William never met her; she died the year before we married. From the time I took up acting, Hathers claimed that she felt less 'useful'. She took up knitting for a while and made an enormous number of extra-wide scarves. They were knitted in a coarse Aran wool that she had bought as a job lot when the wool shop in our town closed down. Although she never progressed past knit-one, purl-one, she discovered a way of increasing the number of stitches in the middle rows to such an extent that the finished article was like a massive cummerbund. Despite my taking a great deal of care in disguising the discomfort of wearing an itchy four-foot-wide scarf, Hathers seemed to know that I didn't want any more of her knitted offerings. I was driven out twice a week to see her, and each week she would have a new scarf ready for me. I suppose I owe my acting to her as well, because I used to act out scenes from films for her to help her understand them. I was Susan Hayward and Elizabeth Taylor and James Dean. I played all the major roles up in the nursery, and I adored it. Even Mummy used to like my acting. We always played charades at Christmas and 'In the Manner of the Word' when we had weekend guests. Long before I had dinner downstairs with her, I used to be called down especially to join in these games. Upstairs, though, Hathers used to dress me up in shawls, and that was best.

I missed Hathers when she died, badly. I missed all her silly habits and the wonderful things she said. I missed the security and the *non sequiturs*, the never knowing where a conversation would turn next, but knowing that there was always someone on my side, whatever that side might be. I was away on location in Spain when Hathers died of flu, but I believe her last words were, 'I shall ask God about the Marx Brothers.'

VI

Rosalind

In my tenth year, with my communion classes looming ever more prominently in my life, Father Ingot was still pressing for a confession. I had read, in one of the musty smuggled tomes from the downstairs library, that the penalty for not answering a charge of high treason was at one time pressing to death. Thus, a man was charged and, if he refused to plead either way, he was fed on enough bread and water to keep him alive, while an iron weight was put on his body. The victim would lie on a stone floor, and each day, he would be called on to speak out. If he refused, the iron weight was increased, until the squashed person either died or confessed. Now Father Ingot seemed to be adopting a new version of this method with me. Bearing down on me with the full weight of his sanctity.

After a further discreet round of questions to one of the girls at the communion class and then, separately, to one of the boys there, I was satisfied by the truth of my Uncle Bertie's statements. I had read, in this same book of ancient torments, that a father might voluntarily choose to be pressed to death rather than plead and have his estates confiscated to the crown. I imagined myself, pinned under the weight of my Uncle Bertie, and oppressed by Father Ingot's unrelenting gaze, yet choosing bravely to remain silent, to protect my family from shame.

So I wore my white silk dress with the Flanders lace and walked up the aisle of St Mary's Church with the other children of my age, and we knelt, and were blessed, and we received the body of Christ into our bodies through the Eucharist. And we were told of the privilege this was. Then I went home, undressed, and changed into my dungarees. Uncle Bertie, who was down for the ceremony, sought me out to hide with him, and I received his body too; but I had a new hope of salvation. I had only to pray for my periods to start, and then he would leave me alone. He himself had said periods were unclean and that they made a child not fit to touch until she was purified again by marriage. I longed for the dirtiness to come. I would lock myself in the bathroom and scrub his touches away, and pray for this soiling of my underpants that alone could save me from the other stickiness.

I played less and less with the village children. I seemed to hide so much and to have so much to hide that there was scarcely time for playing. I read my Bible a lot, and spent many manic hours poised over my jigsaws. I had become prey to a number of irrational fears. I had discovered a way of forgetting all the things that hurt with my uncle, and remembering only the pleasant fizzy moments and the occasional feelings of well-being that came to me when he hugged me very close. Then the nightmares began, forcing me to relive over and over again the things that I didn't want to remember. I would waken from these bad dreams of stallions, aching all over, worse even than I could ache with my uncle. Then I would lie in bed and imagine how one day I might be beatified like Saints Beatrice and Teresa for the sacrifices that I made and for my forbearance. One day, I told myself, my terrible goodness would be recognized and people would tell me that I was right.

I had found a text in the vestry. It was just one from among a whole pile of dog-eared yellow texts, but it seemed appropriate for me. Whenever I felt my eyes sting and the strange feeling of helplessness sinking into me, I would re-read it: 'Obey them that have the rule over you, and submit yourselves: for they watch for your souls, as they that must give account, that they do it with joy, and not with grief . . .'

1962 was a bad year. There must have been some good things about it, but I can't remember a single one. It all seemed bad. My rabbit died in his hutch of some mysterious disease, and the apples in the orchard fell before their time and were ruined. Our nursery oven backfired in Hathers's face one afternoon when she was testing a chocolate cake with a knitting needle, and it singed her eyebrows. Gale-force winds sunk a boat in Hope Bay off the coast not far from us, and the Channel ferries were cancelled for several days. Then, as though by some divine hand, the wood shed in the garden was blown down, and hurled, in its entirety, into the horses' field, where it splintered into a pile of rotten planks. The destruction of this wood shed was the most frightening thing that had ever happened to me. It was my first realization that I was not the only one to live in a network of lies. Despite all Uncle Bertie's claims, and all Father Ingot's texts, I knew by that one sweep of avenging wind that God did not approve of what we did. If he had approved, he would have saved the shed, protected it from the storm, not destroyed it. When Mummy and the others disovered us and were so clearly shocked, it was never as bad as that first divine disapproval. They could only put me in the doghouse and stare their disappointed stares; but God had the power to throw me into hell-fire, and worse still, he could prevent me from becoming a saint.

The implications of the storm seemed endless. I grew thin worrying about them. I had already grown thin before, but now a doctor was called to attend me. He prescribed some vitamin B, a mineral tonic, and a few days in bed. I went to confession regularly, but now I began to breathe desperately through the grill, 'I have sinned, Father,' and yet be unable to put my sin into words; I just knew it was there, like smog or plastic glue, clinging to me in a sickening film. I tried to tell him, and Mummy, and even Hathers again, that I was hiding and hiding was bad. Mummy said that if Uncle Bertie told me to hide, then it was all right and not to worry. But the worry had come to stay. Later, when the door to the loft room burst open, and Mummy called out, I felt almost relieved.

'What on earth are you doing, Bertie?' she said. And then she caught sight of me, naked underneath him. Mummy and Hathers were stuck in the doorway; they looked as if they could move neither backwards nor forwards. For some reason, Uncle Jeremey was with them, and he was the one to move. He came and hit Uncle Bertie in the face, and pushed him off me, and then he grabbed for me, and I thought he was going to hit me too, so I covered my face and begged him not to. Seeing me cowering like that, he must have thought that Bertie used to hit me. I felt confused, since he had only spanked me once, and I think he slapped me a few times, but only when I was being difficult.

A doctor was called, our doctor, and he examined me in my nightie, and did the same things that my uncle used to do. He said it was all right, just as Uncle Bertie had, so I really thought everyone would be doing it now, and Uncle Bertie had been right after all. Mummy was with me in the room, and she was weeping, but she wouldn't talk, and she wouldn't quite look at me.

The doctor said, 'You can thank God, Mrs Palliser, she's all right. Nothing has happened.'

Then they left me. As they went out of the door, I heard the doctor say, 'When you think what might have happened, you've been very lucky . . . just in time. A terrible business.'

I lay in bed, watching Hathers bustling around the room, re-arranging my underclothes in my chest of drawers and turning her singed face towards me every few seconds in appeal. I felt that she wanted me to rally and take the lead again, as I always did, so I suggested some tea, and she went gratefully to make it.

For years afterwards, I wondered what this other thing that might have happened could have been. I wondered too how they could call my years in the wood shed 'nothing'. And I wondered why I was simultaneously thus saved and condemned. Mummy refused to mention the subject again. As for Uncle Bertie, long after he had gone back to Australia, we still didn't mention his name. Our whole family history was rewritten without him. It was as though he and the memory of him had slipped into the fourth dimension. I used to imagine him, like one of Columbus's sailors, falling over the edge of the earth into space. It occurred to me that, somewhere out in New South Wales, little Australian girls were being taught to hide, as I had been. I hoped, for their sakes, that they reached their puberty undiscovered by any shocked outsiders. The being caught seemed worse almost than what I had done. What had I done? What had I done wrong?

Gradually, like my mother, I found it all too traumatic and I began to block it out. For years I treated my relationship with Uncle Bertie as though it were just another film I'd seen. The only thing to distinguish it from those hundreds of films was that it was the one plot we never discussed in the nursery, the one script that Hathers never asked me to explain.

Sometimes as a child I used to go to the beach, to Folkestone mostly, but sometimes elsewhere. I used to help Hathers collect coloured glass. She had a magpie-like obsession with the stuff. She used to be content to scour the sands for hours on end, bobbing down to pick up a flash of green or red or, rarest of all, blue. There was a number of big jars in the nursery which gradually filled with these rounded scraps, worn and left by the sea. As a child, I used to gather useless bits of information and treasure them like Hathers with her glass. I discovered a Victorian gentleman who feared that his backside was made of glass and that the slightest knock or jolt would shatter it. I compared his fate to the saints and martyrs and was amazed at how much some people needed to suffer, myself included.

Long after Uncle Bertie had disappeared, and long after I had ceased waiting for an antipodean postcard to explain to me what I had done wrong, or even just to say hello, I tormented myself with feelings of remorse and guilt. I began to read the accounts of trials and to re-read the lives of the martyrs and I imagined myself on their racks and consumed by their flames. I would lock myself in the lavatory and weep in silent hysteria for the anguish of Lady Jane Grey or the courage of some unknown warrior. I cried for them, and for myself, and I longed for someone else to cry with me.

I read with horror and fascination about the hangings and the suicides of fallen women. They were defiled, and I was defiled. I dreamt of lying in state on the long marble tomb down in our church, where the effigies of a fifteenth-century lord of the manor and his wife lay carved in alabaster. I dreamt of the parish coming to pay their respects and of my mother repenting her absence and her failure to understand my needs. And I imagined that Uncle Jeremy, who had hauled me so harshly from the attic mattress, knelt and wept. In real life Uncle Jeremy had developed a way of not quite looking me in the eye and muttering something about my being a 'poor old thing' when he saw me. He'd give me a shilling and tell me to go back to Hathers, as though Hathers had the power to protect me. Even Uncle Bertie would appear in this dream, dragged back from the Pacific in chains to weep for me, and, as he passed my wasted corpse, he would lean over and whisper 'I forgive you' and I would almost feel my dead flesh smile at the sweetness of this release. Then Hathers would come, sobbing and choking as she did uncontrollably when she cried. I would try to make her stand sedately towards the back of the church, dressed in black and merely clutching the pew end for strength. But Hathers's grief knew no bounds, even in my dream, and, for as much as I tried to rearrange the set, I couldn't stop her sobbing. So I would always have to wake up and deal with the reality of the cold morning or the dark night. I couldn't leave her to cry alone. She seemed to need me more than I needed the apologies and the praise.

Over the years, though, I always needed that praise. Never a day passed that I didn't need to reaffirm my goodness and my good looks and my power to be liked. William used to say that he couldn't understand how anyone as beautiful and successful as myself could be so insecure. Half the time I don't understand it myself. But it's there. I was told that the Hays Code used to insist right up until 1958 that the male in every love scene screened in America had to keep one foot on the floor at all times. It struck me, later, that I made love like that too, with something always held back, always tied down, made artificially and almost ridiculously difficult.

Perhaps that was what first attracted me to Candy when she came to be interviewed as a nanny: her vanity and her ravenous need to conquer. I felt a kind of instant affinity with her. William was horrified by my choice. 'What can this daily beauty queen offer our two silent girls? It must take her hours to make up her face every day – what time would there be over for the twins?' I knew from the start that William would never really understand Candy, but that I did. Just as no one had ever been able to appreciate Hathers, except for me. Sometimes a kind of ineptitude is helpful in a job. The twins needed their own freedom to develop. Nothing that anyone did, other than be kind, feed and clothe them, could really penetrate to them until they themselves were ready. I thought that Candy would not smother them with unwanted attention, while, at the same time, she would remain nominally in charge. I recognized that she was probably incapable of the more mundane tasks such as making tea and tidying up the nursery, but there was always Mrs King, the workaholic, to do those things. I think really that it was more the discovery of a desperate feminine spirit, caught in its own dilemma, that made me take Candy into the household and then keep her there for so many years. It was actually only five years, but they seemed like a lifetime, counting the days and the wrinkles and equating flattery with guile.

William used to say sometimes, 'That girl is absolutely useless! She never does a single stroke of work.'

I knew that Candy would have resented that, and denied it, because she worked sometimes like a slave. It was just that Willie couldn't see how hard she strived, or understand the energy needed to turn a man's head every day.

Most women who have been in love or even felt an attraction for someone have felt that kind of inner panic that comes with it. Not so many, though, have that predatory streak that drives them out on to the streets to hunt and tease. It sounds like simple prostitution put like that, but it's an urge that stops where prostitution begins. When I tried once to explain this to William, he found it very hard to comprehend, not least because he couldn't understand why I should want to share my house with a rival. In practice, there was no rivalry between Candy and me: she wanted bodies, and I wanted minds. Once in a while I still have to test my skill, pitching myself against a total stranger, captivating him for an hour or a day or a week, and then I don't want to be reminded of my weakness. I'd like all the victims of my experiments to disappear. Working was the worst time because these old conquests kept being cast beside me. There was a cameraman on my second film who had a tremendous repertoire of *risqué* stories. He was called Tony but he liked to be called Tone. The director used to say that you could rely on him to lower the tone of every set he was on, but that he was a brilliant cameraman. Tone had an obsession with Catherine the Great; he told me that, when she was Empress, she used to choose lovers from among her guards, have them brought up to her, spend a night with them and then let them out through a back door. He claimed that they were all executed on their way out.

I used to get very bored filming. Half the time I thought it was because I didn't have much to say to the rest of the cast, and, being both shy and arrogant, I successfully kept most of them from getting to know me. I lived in a dream that was frequently inaccessible to myself, let alone outsiders. One day, though, there was a hitch while we were filming a very moving farewell. The shooting was stopped for a few minutes while the problem was sorted out, and Tone moved in close to me and began to whisper an outrageous story about Catherine the Great dying while trying to have intercourse with a horse. I thought of Hathers and her horses and of the old stallion in our village back home and the sweet-shop lady who kept him, and suddenly I began to laugh. The shooting recommenced, the sad parting came, and in the middle of it, I was seized by a fit of laughter so uncontrollable I had to be taken back to my hotel. Until then, I had forgotten how to laugh. Afterwards, I vowed never to forget again. It turned me from an embittered introvert into a potential friend. I think that hailed the end of feeling bored – the end of an era.

VII

William

Why did you go to Larenguebec? We came to Sestri Levante because you saw the name on the map and liked it, but Larenguebec isn't on the map, and I don't think you'd ever heard of it before, nobody seemed to have heard of it. Then a friend of a friend came round to see us at Tanza Road, and mentioned that desolate stretch of Normandy and an empty house there that he had rented but wouldn't use. I wondered at the time why he didn't stay there himself – I know now. You became very excited about it, and took the house from him unseen. What was the allure of that abandoned beach with nothing but sand and stone and discontent wedged into its disproportionate harbour?

After this so-called friend had left, I said, 'Why go there, Rosalind?'

'Why go anywhere?' you said, and shrugged, and I recognized your old restlessness taking hold of you.

There were long periods when you seemed to glaze over, and others when you would just disappear. You had been unsettled for some months, and it was I who suggested that you take a holiday on your own, by the sea. I had nothing to lose; you had become impenetrable, at least to me. A seaside resort was one thing, but why go to Larenguebec?

At the last minute, I contemplated trying to hold you back, detain you by some devious means. When I tried to dissuade you, I don't think you could even hear me. You were locked in some incurable indifference. I had seen you like it before; when the twins were born, and later when Amadeo was so nearly stillborn. You had emerged from the hospital, a monster of indifference, and then, as now, you would look out to sea, scanning the horizon for someone or something you missed. You lived in a state of orchestrated lack; when there was no sea you would invent it.

Outside in the singed and overgrown garden, the twins were playing in the weeds. Amadeo, aged two, was sitting under a japonica bush, clutching the bemused tortoise. I watched you staring out through the sash windows at the children, and I sensed that you saw something very different from me. The twins looked up. They had an uncanny way of doing things in unison like a variety act. They caught sight of you and smiled with that strange, almost sinister, smile they had. They began to chant,

> 'I scream, *you* scream,
> We all scream for ice cream!'

Then came their customary howl, a desperate strangled cry that used to hurt my head. They made it sound as though you were at the core of their own manic behaviour. Our house was like a madhouse again.

During that early summer, though, when the sun never seemed to go in even over Hampstead Heath and Tanza Road, you had begun to crave solitude. Before that, you had always clung to me; so much, in fact, that sometimes it was I who would rise early and walk across the Heath just to be alone for a while. Then you began to grow desperate to get away. The house had begun to fill with irrational fears for you. Several times I had found you weeping in the bathroom. You claimed the noises of the house perturbed you. The occasional traffic outside, the shrieking of the twins, Candy's inane stream of chatter, Mrs King forever complaining and Amadeo practising his thirty words like never-ending scales. 'Bye bye sea, bye bye car, bye bye sea.' These were the parameters of his existence, ground into the household, hour after hour.

So you latched on to the idea of Larenguebec, and you began to prepare for your journey. Although I'd suggested it, it seemed suddenly unfair of you to exclude me from your travel. We had always been together – always being ten years. I never wanted to force you into anything, so when you said you had to go alone, I helped you as best I could and tried not to show my rejection. But when I saw that you intended to travel with your customary circus, I was so annoyed, I just let you get on with it.

If I try to date the beginning of my exclusion from the household, I suppose it would be from the time that the twins chose to talk, which was the time of Amadeo's birth. It was as though I were an outsider in a girls' dormitory. You shared treats and secrets: you and Candy and the twins, making an exception for the androgynous Amadeo. I sometimes felt like the enemy. Only Amadeo, dressed in frills of white lace, with his halo of long curls, accepted me. He managed with his smile to make me an honorary girl, like him.

That isn't altogether true. You accepted me too, when you wished to. There would be days when I was Willie or Jimmy or the football fan, and I was yours; but there would also be days when you would look at me and through your silence I could hear you wondering, 'And who are you?'

The linguistically gifted twins, who were a source of amazement at their school, and who brought child assessors and child psychiatrists down from all over Greater London the better to measure their skills, could be very cruel. Perhaps they were more relentless than cruel, since it wasn't so much what they said or did, as their obsessional insistence.

One afternoon they came back from school suddenly fired with an enthusiasm for geography. They seemed to want to establish a personal connection with every country that there was. They delved into our family histories.

'Yes, but where was your great-grandmother born?'

'And where did your Uncle Jeremy go to school?'

'Is there anyone from Hampshire?'

There was no one, and Florence or Hattie was nearly moved to tears. They each wore a little locket on a gold chain round their neck, engraved with their name. Thus one said 'Florence' and the other 'Harriet', but we had long established that they swapped these tags and so they would always have to be just twins. The twins this and the twins that, and when only one of them was required, you would say to Candy, bring me a twin. Even their cuts and bruises came in duplicate. If one girl burnt herself, then the other would match the burn. They marked themselves cut for cut, so that no tell-tale scar should distinguish one from the other. That afternoon of the English counties, though, only one of them had tears in her eyes. Within seconds, the tears were gone and the twins were back in unison, but now with a kind of vicious urgency.

'So Mummy is Kent and Daddy is Cumbria/Norfolk.'

They smiled at each other and then began to chant,

> 'The Cumbrian Walsh or mountain sheep
> Is of the Ovine race.
> His conversation is not deep
> But then observe his face.'

We all laughed; it was cleverly done, to turn this rhyme to my name. But even through the laughter, they had started again, and all through the remainder of the afternoon they chanted. They were banished to the back garden, where they chanted in the grass. Then they chanted through the walls of their bedroom. I don't know why a few words repeated over and over can have such a strange effect. They made me feel dizzy, almost sick.

It was a long summer, and we were all tired. I hadn't realized how tired I was until you began to pack and I to see that maybe I needed a rest as much as you did, and maybe the separation would be for the best. I trusted your instincts, and I blame myself now for that. I didn't realize how unwell you were. I thought you were trying to take an elaborate holiday, I didn't realize you were struggling to survive. If you surrounded yourself with all that was most familiar, you did so from a need, not a caprice. And, though you took all the girls, you were not responsible, not fit, not able to look after them. It was you who needed looking after, you who needed the help.

You took them all with you, though, that potentially lethal human zoo, as though in your inner loneliness you found security in clutter. Even with hindsight I find it hard to understand how you chose to move with that troupe of girls ranging from delayed adolescence through the various stages of precocious delinquency and charm. I discovered, later, that you even drugged the cat and put it in the picnic basket, and you smuggled Fred the tortoise across the Channel in a hollow compartment of the pram. And Fred was my tortoise too – but then Amadeo was my son.

You were all travelling by train from Waterloo. It was, of course, the height of the tourist season, and the station was insufferably inundated with people and luggage, and most of the luggage seemed to be yours. You had suitcases and bags, the picnic basket, a Saratoga trunk, another, smaller trunk and countless miscellaneous packages all assembled round Amadeo's pram. The twins wanted drinks and buns, which I volunteered to buy at a kiosk, but you preferred to take them into the cafeteria, where you billeted your party in the few empty chairs. The twins had found out how to blow bubbles through a straw in a glass, and they were noisily demonstrating this somewhere behind us. I had a cup of tea, while you and Amadeo had a plate of toast and jam. On the far side of the mirrored room, Candy was making an early kill with a middle-aged commuter.

On certain days you would become intrigued with the nature of things. This was one of those days, and it was the toast that fascinated you. You became suddenly obsessed by its texture, its tastelessness and, I suppose, the fact that it existed at all. Amadeo, who had only recently recovered from a chest infection, was coughing beside you, and I was trying to remind you of his tendency to asthma, and his infuriating stoicism in the face of pain. Despite his still uncompleted two years, he never complained, but just stared dully, as though across the stillness of an imaginary lake, and slept more than was normal.

So Amadeo coughed, and I fussed, and you analysed the nature of your toast and its apparent relevance to the day.

'Perhaps we should make our way to the train now?' I said hopefully.

'What's it made of?' you asked, for the third time, holding up a brittle, charred slice of British Rail toast.

'What's one supposed to do with it?'

Amadeo, temporarily released from his chair, had found his own solution to this problem. He had spread raspberry jam on the toast, and was intent on wiping it off across neighbouring table tops and people's knees. Our part of the cafeteria was beginning to take on the aspect of a quarantine ship, with a kind of voluntary cordon drawn round it as the volume of protests grew. Only Candy, in the seventh circle of her flirtation, and you, with your Hathers-like interest in the toast, didn't seem to notice. I myself had long grown beyond embarrassment, trained by the twins to forbear squalor and

70

shame. I ushered you all, protesting, on to the station forecourt, and then I took you to the train.

After you'd left for Portsmouth and the ferry, I began to hate Larenguebec. I'd helped a porter to load your luggage and the pram into the guard's van, and then I'd watched you go, staring, it seemed, almost desperately out through your grimy, closed window. Even on the platform, five minutes before the train was due to leave, I had offered to go with you, and to see you installed safely on your unmapped beach. You spoke to me then, with a defensive urgency.

'I need to hide on my own,' you said, 'where there will be fishing boats and warm bread.'

How do you hide with three extravagant females in your wake and an overgrown baby? I was piqued by the reference to the bread. We had warm bread in Tanza Road, bought fresh every day from the bakery at South End Green. Then you gripped my arm, and I remember that you dug your hard nails in so far that it hurt.

'I have to go,' you repeated. 'I have got to get away.'

And you went, Rosalind, away to a wasteland, and I still don't know what inner force drove you there, or what inner fear dragged you into the attic at Larenguebec and kept you there, hiding in the dark, on your own. Nor do I know how long you had been like that, hiding. You were gone for four weeks, but I don't know how soon the trouble began.

I've pieced together what I can, from you, from the twins, and from my own trip to France after their phone call. I know that you sailed to Cherbourg, and I can imagine the ferry trip out. It will have been like the cafeteria at Waterloo only three times worse. There was no one to move you on as I always did, like a bunch of vagrants disturbing the peace. It always rains at Portsmouth: a kind of fine sprinkling as one steps up the gangplank to the ferry. You once suggested that the French Tourist Board paid a sailor to open a hose so that all the holidaymakers could see what a good time it was to be leaving England. I expect it rained for you. I hope you had the presence of mind to put the pram in with the cars and not try to force it up the gangplank and across the crowded decks, but I don't know.

I missed you terribly while you were away. I even missed all the bad things about the twins. I thought that Fred and the cat had pined and run off. I didn't realize that you had taken them too, but the house seemed desolate without you. Mrs King, with a kind of prophetic insistence, kept worrying about Amadeo's cough.

'I hope Her Nibs is all right,' she'd say, ominously, about you; and then add primly, 'A fat lot of good that bit of Candy is going to be with poor little Amidy and his cough.' I couldn't tell whether Mrs King genuinely couldn't grasp the baby's name, or whether she just disapproved of its foreignness, but she never did get it right. I sent you a stream of letters and telegrams to that forlorn address; you never sent so much as one. I knew that you didn't like writing letters, so I didn't particularly worry. When I went out to Larenguebec, I found my letters heaped up unopened, gathering dust inside the door. I wrote to Candy too, and to the twins. I think the twins read their cards, but Candy's were all with yours on the floor.

That summer was unnaturally hot. I felt listless and I could hardly sleep. I got a lot of work done, forcing myself to finish all my backlog and even to rough out posters for my two new contracts, which were, I remember, a lipstick and a new wax cleaner. Strange things were happening, even in England. Swarms of greenfly had hatched and gathered finger-deep in the garden. Some days there would be a brittle carpet of ladybirds on the step. The geraniums in Amadeo's nursery died. There had been pelargoniums and ordinary geraniums and a scented rose geranium that was said to keep flies off. He always liked flowers, particularly the reds and pinks of these 'lows' as he called them. I thought of him seeing their fallen petals and scorched leaves and alternating his habitual 'Bye bye car, bye bye sea' with a new 'Bye bye flower' and somehow I couldn't bring myself to clear them away, or to let the fanatical Mrs King do so.

You had arranged to return exactly four weeks after your departure, which would have been 10 September, ten days before Amadeo's birthday, and just two days before the beginning of term. The twins called me on the fourth (Saint Rosalia the Virgin's Day, I believe). It was a strange call with a bad line and an irate operator cutting in all the time. There was no telephone in the house at Larenguebec, and I didn't know then where they were calling from, or how. The sound of their voices seemed far more distant than the

72

Channel's breadth away, almost spectral. It was hardly more than a croak when I heard it, and it frightened me. They spoke in a babyish voice that was not their own, 'I need to speak to William Walsh.' I kept telling them that it was me, but it was as though they couldn't hear me, or didn't recognize my voice. Then one of them said, 'Please ask him to come.'

There was a long silence from them, filled by a distant hissing on the line and my own reassurances and enquiries. They ignored everything I said for a while, then they began to interrupt in a dull monotone, 'Are you there, are you there, are we talking?'

I called them by their nursery names, Tiddly and Floss, and adopted their own tactic of repetition.

'Floss, Floss, what's the matter?'

There was another silence, then, 'Somebody has to come for Mummy . . . and the pram.'

They sounded very matter of fact. I waited for them to say something else, but there was just another unnerving silence. I thought the line had gone dead, so I called out, 'Hello, hello, Tiddly, Floss—'

A voice said, 'It's a grey house.'

It didn't sound like their voice, then the flat 'disconnected' tone began, and I knew either we had been cut off or they had hung up. I waited by the telephone for several minutes to see if they would ring back. Then I phoned a travel agent, and began to pack. I remember feeling secretly pleased that you all still needed me: had I known why, I suppose I would have wept.

VIII
William

None of the taxi-drivers wanted to go to Larenguebec. I was more irritated than alarmed by the number of men who refused to take me there. I calculated that it was about fifty kilometres from Cherbourg, where I stayed the night. I took it more as a general failure of the *Entente Cordiale* than a reflection on Larenguebec, when, one after another, the drivers turned me down. I stomped around the Place du Théâtre, recalling bitterly the days before Britain joined the Common Market, when the butter came from New Zealand, and taxi-drivers on the Continent were a lot more civil. I offered one driver double the fare to take me there, but he only crossed himself and shook his head. There were no cars left to hire, and the tourists were everywhere, sweltering in the steadily increasing heat.

I wandered back towards the docks, and paused *en route* to rethink my plans over a late breakfast at the Hôtel de Paris. Over my second cup of coffee, I asked the waiter where I could find a taxi that would go to Larenguebec. He smiled, knowingly, and said, in French, 'Only Pierre Laurent goes there now.' He flicked some crumbs from my table with a linen cloth. 'He lost a brother there, but he still goes back, sometimes. He is scared of it now.'

Nobody else in the whole of Cherbourg had even been prepared to recognize the existence of Larenguebec. I felt strangely grateful to this waiter for discussing it with me. He was a young man in his mid-twenties, and he had very intense, deep-set black eyes and immaculate, almost navy-blue, hair. It seemed that I had triggered some memory for him that took him from his immediate surroundings of restaurant and white linen table-cloths to some hidden disturbance in his past.

'I knew a girl from there once,' he said staring vaguely through me at the blank wall behind. Then he paused, and the ensuing silence grew uneasy.

'Yes . . .?' I encouraged him.

But he continued to stare. Then he shuddered involuntarily and shook himself from his trance. He looked suddenly embarrassed, and began to brush the crumbs nervously from my table-cloth. Then he stopped, as abruptly as he had started, and assumed once more his cool professional stance.

'Don't go there,' he said, in a tone of voice that could have easily said, 'Don't have the beef bourguignon tonight.' 'It is a bad place,' he added firmly and took the saucer from under my raised cup, as though to imply that the conversation and my breakfast were now over. I gulped down the last of my coffee before his stern hand returned to take that too.

'I have to go there,' I told him, shrugging half-apologetically, and then hurried on, before he could display all his expressions of disdain. 'Will this driver Laurent take me?'

'Oh, yes,' he said, 'he went only last month to take an English-woman there.'

'Why is it a bad place?' I asked him.

He bent suddenly towards my table, eager, it seemed, to tell me. Then something crossed his mind and shadowed his dark eyes, and he thought better of it; stood back and prepared to leave.

'There is the Centrale,' he half-whispered.

'What Centrale?' I asked.

'Five years ago the Government built a nuclear reactor there, just outside the village. Before it happened, demonstrators came in from all over Europe. We had the Green Party from Germany, we had the whole works.'

'And?'

'And they showed what would happen if this Centrale came. Radiation sickness, deformed babies, dead crops, the lot. They showed films and stuck posters all over Normandy.'

'So what happened?'

'Well,' the waiter said, clearing his throat slightly, and flicking another crumb from my table. 'The people who came to demon-strate were so undesirable, all the locals thought that anything these druggy layabouts with safety-pins in their noses and green hair

75

didn't want must be good. So they all voted for it. The locals welcomed the Centrale as a way of scaring off these hordes of camping bearded nomads.'

I finished my coffee and he took my cup.

'Now,' he added, 'that Centrale smells like the Devil himself – and the place is full of Arabs.'

I listened attentively, nodding from time to time, but no more.

'All they had to say was: if you have this Centrale, it'll be manned by Arabs, and the Arabs will want to drink in your bars. Aah . . .' he laughed scornfully. 'Why talk of ecology to fishermen? Ecology *merde*! Now Larenguebec has grown violent, strange – they're all scared of it now.'

'Has there been a leak then?' I asked, but he wasn't going to tell me. He wheeled round and walked away. I called out after his receding back, 'And Larent's phone number?'

He turned now and half-bowed.

'It is in the book, *monsieur.*'

I found that the telephone number was indeed in the book, but rather as a pebble is in the sea; for the Pierre, Pascal and Paul Laurents of Cherbourg all denied any knowledge of the man. It was only after what must have been my thirtieth call that a certain Orfelie Laurent told me that her brother-in-law, Jean-Pierre, did indeed have a taxi and the number was listed under J. Laurent. I rang it, and within minutes the man himself pulled up to the kerb in front of me in a scratched but gleaming Citroën.

It was one of those days when the temperature seems to defy any normal scale of measurement. Sometimes, before a storm, the same kind of sultry heat and oppressive atmosphere can seem literally to pin one down, and drain away every last scrap of energy. I don't know if there was a storm gathering somewhere along that Normandy coast, or if, in the days after we left, any thunder came to clear the air, but that morning it felt like an alien force. Even had there been nothing else to contend with, the heat alone was enough to break my spirit. The town of Cherbourg had been protecting us from the full glare of the sun, and it was only when we reached the open road that I felt there was something exaggerated about the weather.

Jean-Pierre Laurent, my driver, was a man in his sixties, thick set and squat. His fingers were so short that they scarcely gripped the nylon leopard-skin cover of the steering-wheel. He had the blue watery eyes of a man prone either to excessive weeping or to drink. The network of broken purple capillaries across his face seemed to point to the latter. Perhaps, though, the most noticeable thing about him was his compulsive talking. From the moment I entered the car until the end of the journey there was an almost ceaseless flow of talk. He seemed neither to need nor heed his audience; his monologue had a relentless insistence. The heat of the day, the man's incessant babble and its detrimental effect on his driving all combined to make my journey out to Larenguebec a kind of surreal odyssey.

He remembered you, Rosalind, he referred to you as 'the lady with the strange eyes', and he told me in his clear coastal French how he had enjoyed sitting next to you for the half-hour ride when he took you out, those weeks before, to Larenguebec. He explained to me that he had been feeling '*nerveux*' the day he drove you, and the thought of going out to Larenguebec had filled him with dread, but that your presence had somehow calmed him down. I warmed to Laurent for understanding these things about you. He seemed nervous again, though, with me.

I found his French surprisingly easy to follow and I sat back and listened while he regaled me with stories about Cherbourg and the world in general. He paid very scant attention to the road and seemed quite unmoved by the frequency with which he nearly collided with other cars. His own scratched Citroën appeared to be self propelled, so smoothly did it glide between oncoming traffic, pedestrians, and obstacles of all kinds. Once in a while I would lose the drift of his conversation when I turned away to unstick my spine from the blue plastic covering of the car seat, but after a while I gave up battling with the sweat and heat and he had my full attention. He told me how impressed he had been with the way you handled the children, seeming to anticipate their needs telepathically.

'Then,' he said sadly, 'I came back and heard how that poor baby had been locked all night in a wardrobe on his own.' He shook his head, and added, 'The morning maid nearly died of fright when she went in with the breakfast tray; and out of that empty room a piercing cry had come from that wardrobe. She dropped the tray and ran.' He turned and looked at me hard, as though I had been an accomplice in what he saw as this inquitious neglect. I kept my face suitably blank, and refrained from explaining how Amadeo actually liked constrained dark spaces, and was incapable of sleeping anywhere else. I knew that he had to sleep alone. He would wake and cry all night if his usual, almost narcoleptic, sleep was interrupted. And I knew that we had often made him a mattress of pillows inside a capacious cupboard, when travelling, in the absence of a cot in a quiet room. I realized that it would be impossible to explain this to my shocked driver.

'What kind of a mother would do such a thing?' he asked. I was in the throes of composing a reply in passable French when he leapt on to the next subject.

'It was as though something made her go there. I took to her, though. I felt that if I were to line her up against my sister-in-law Orfelie, the lady with the strange eyes would win.' He turned to me here and winked. 'Nobody else in the whole world could bend my sister's will.' He cleared his throat and wiped the sweat from his brow. 'The baby carriage scraped the paint off my car. I didn't want to charge her for it, but . . . even if she had been the blessed Virgin herself . . . a man has to live.'

He shrugged and we drove on in a brief silence interspersed by his almost rhythmical repetition of the name Orfelie, he made it sound like 'awfully', which, combined with the dread in his voice as he said it, had a strangely sobering effect on me.

We were well away now from the prim shuttered rows of houses and the outlying estates of modern flats. On either side of the road, mixed hedges straggled into small, well-tended fields interrupted by the occasional hamlet of grey stone houses. It was still unnaturally hot, and it seemed to be getting hotter. As we passed through St Sauveur the taxi swerved to avoid a group of conscripts who looked as though their feet had melted into the tarmac. My driver whistled angrily through his teeth.

'Some people like trouble.'

I nodded.

'They look for it,' he said.

Again I agreed politely.

'That wife of yours, she is like that,' he smiled with a mixture of distress and admiration.

We drove on faster now, as though to prove that he too could be reckless when he chose. I felt like telling him that I needed no proof of his prowess behind the wheel, I was already impressed, but I couldn't squeeze a word into his own barrage of talk.

'Orfelie is a formidable woman too,' he told me. I smiled with what I hoped implied reciprocal approval. 'Not like that, though,' he told me, wagging his finger virtually under my nose, while the car, with his hands thus freed from the wheel, swerved across the road. I dropped my smile abruptly, and stumbled into an apology, explaining that nothing 'like that' had been intended. He swept aside my effusive 'pardons' and launched into his own line of questioning.

'What do you think of when you hear that name, Orfelie?' he demanded.

I tried to ignore my recent forebodings at his strange repetition of it, and conjured up instead visions from Shakespeare and Millais.

'Fragility?' I hazarded.

'When I think of Orfelie, I think dragon,' he said. 'Orfelie: dragon. My sister-in-law, she has stolen the meaning of her name. She has taken, always taken. My brother went to Larenguebec because he couldn't stand her any more. They called it an industrial accident, but it was like suicide. He died to get away from her. The dragon,' he repeated, and laughed bitterly. Then he relaxed. 'That lady of yours, why did she go to Larenguebec?'

I found myself repeating your phrase, 'Why go anywhere?'

He shrugged again and continued, 'Yes, yes, but Larenguebec, ever since they put the nuclear plant there, it is not the same place.' He seemed to gather his fat in closer to him to protect him from his fears. 'It is not what it seems. For five years now there is something bad there, you can feel it in the air. The Centrale, everything. It isn't safe for her – not for those girls either.' I sat back uneasily. I had started to feel sick. We passed a road sign to Carentan.

'The people, they are riff-raff, not even French,' he said, jerking the car right to avoid Carentan, 'they're Arabs. If it weren't for the crabs, God knows what there would be found floating in the sea.'

'Crabs?' I repeated, holding back a wave of nausea as the taxi charged yet another hill in third gear.

'That's what they used to fish for.'

'Used to?'

'There's hardly anyone left now, of the old lot, and those that are left are fishing for trouble.' The driver himself was impressed into momentary silence, then the spectre of the sea came into view over the hill, and he shuddered. His voice seemed to break loose again, insinuating its way into my innermost thoughts like a fraying rope of spume dragging at the sand.

Between the pressure of my seat belt and the sticky plastic of my seat, I felt that I was being held in a dream. Outside Cherbourg, when we passed the first ribbon of grey stone cottages – the *boulangerie,* bar, and that straggling line of identical dwellings – it struck me that they were spaced almost as though they were afraid to huddle together. At first that air of semi-regimented despair seemed quaint, but as we passed one hamlet after another, each as grey and as unforgiving as the last, I grew tired of them. Until that half-hour ride to Larenguebec I didn't know I could grow tired of a colour so quickly, and yet the greyness showed me: the walls were grey, and the road, and the gulls and the houses, and the sky, for all its heat, still shimmered grey, and even the skin of the peasants peering out from behind grubby curtains was grey. Only the greens, the oaks and the sycamores, contrasted with the dour twilight shades. By St Sauveur, though, the drone of my driver's voice had so effectively blended with the forced roar of his engine and my own fears as to make me believe that the green itself was a tremendous growth of mould.

When the sea came into view I felt a kind of dizziness grip the back of my head. It was hard to breathe in the heat. The tide was low, and I felt, looking at the sweep of dunes and rock that joined the sea to dry land, that it was pulling and grasping at all it could. It was pulling at me on the hill, at the taxi, at the haze of sand, sucking us into its mysterious depths and giving nothing back. The driver matched my change of mood: where before he had talked from a wish to communicate, he spoke now from a reluctant need to annihilate silence. This time I refused to listen. I had the sea to torment me now, so I blocked out his ramblings about the evils of the nuclear plant and the alleged bandits that ran it. Instead, I dreamt that I had buried my head somewhere in those coves of bleached sand.

Interspersed with all his complaints and comments, the driver kept telling me how desperate you'd seemed when he drove you out. He called it hounded, fretful, scared – he called it all the things that had never really occurred to me about you. Even before I reached Larenguebec, he showed me how ill you were. You had always been so capable, and well, Rosalind. You were capable of dealing with everything, I had believed, from daily chores to deaths. When things displeased you, you ignored them. You always seemed at ease in that sea of *non sequiturs* you lived in. Sometimes I forced myself to think what might have happened if someone else had found you all. What would have happened if an outsider had got to you first? I suppose I blame myself for not having the telepathy to have got there sooner, and saved you some of the misery of the aftermath. Remembering the sea at Larenguebec is like dryland drowning.

It was only meant to be another six kilometres to the house and the taxi was doing a steady fifty, and yet that last lap from the crest of the hill to you was the slowest. I could drown the monologue beside me, but I couldn't ignore the heat. It was like stepping off an aeroplane into the tropics. My ankles were beginning to swell. I remember feeling thankful that Mrs King back in South End Green couldn't see me – she had a neurotic anxiety about eating too much salt. She used to criticize my excessive uses of it, and threaten me with future deposits of albumen around my ankles that would look like elephantiasis. Watching my thin socks stretch transparent over my insteps, I felt disturbed by the accuracy of her prophecies. The air-conditioning appeared to have broken down. I opened the window on my side, but the driver shook his sweating face sadly.

'That'll only make it worse.'

By the time we were approaching the village itself, I realized that the twins' description, 'It's a grey house', was a useless guide to finding it. From our artificial intimacy of the last half-hour Laurent had become suddenly both fierce and distant. Everything about him seemed to be changing, from his tone of voice to the way in which he sat and held the wheel. At the crossroads just outside the village he turned a brooding and newly hostile face to me and insisted that I get out. His violence must have been contagious, because I turned on him with a savagery in my own voice that I'd never heard before. I insisted that he take me to the very house where he had left you. Their description was useless. Grey, everything was grey at Larenguebec, but I knew that he must know where to go in that exposed warren to find you.

One road led to the village and a stark sign pointed along another road to the Centrale, the nuclear plant, and the beach. We climbed a low rise towards you. For once, he was driving slowly. The last lap of the route had smelt of a fishing village with its sour, barnacled odour of stale shellfish and damp nets. I had noticed little piles of dead crabs and their remains outside one or two of the houses. Then we slowed beside a row of three tall cottages standing on their own. The driver had regained some of his former composure, and refused either to stop or get out of the car. He pointed to the middle door of the three dwellings and then demanded two hundred francs. I waited for a moment for him to cut his engine, then I gave up and opened my door. I leant back in, paid him and straightened my hot crumpled clothes. He crossed himself and let the money fall to the taxi floor. I heard him mutter something like a prayer as he drove off up the hill with the car door swinging free.

There were flies everywhere. Outside your door there was a heap of long-dead crabs looking more deliberately gathered or discarded than elsewhere. As I knocked on the door, a wizened face appeared at your neighbour's window. I nodded, and was met by a glacial stare before the face disappeared, and the cobbled net curtain slipped back into place.

Although most of your windows were broken, your door was locked; and the house seemed deserted. At first I was annoyed at not being able to get in. I felt that same irrational anger one feels when phoning a friend and instead of an answer, the telephone just rings and rings. Why were you out when I had come all this way to find you? The moment passed, and I tried the door again to make sure that it was really locked. Then I looked down at my modest holdall, and thanked God that I wasn't travelling with the kind of luggage you always trailed behind you. I made my way back down the hill to the village and the beach. Where else would you be at lunchtime in that heat?

It was a relief to be away from the taxi. There had been something overbearing about the driver's manner. I felt chagrined that a stranger should be the one to draw my attention to your distress. I suppose it was strange that your windows were both broken and barricaded. I supposed I should have wondered right from the start at the darkness and the chaos and the crabs; but I still believed then in a just world. I was brought up a Christian, albeit reluctantly, and good people like you didn't get hurt.

You had always lived in what you called the world of the cleaver, where good things were cut down. You grew up used and abused and neglected; almost starved by affluence. I know you had all that food, as I did too, but where was your mother's love or even time – where was mine? And where was your father? It was almost as if he had fallen off the face of the earth. You never mention him, your mother never mentioned him. I don't even know how he died. Then Hathers died, then your mother and your Uncle Jeremy. I escaped from the regrigerator of my own start to a world of constant warmth and improvement. You must have taken your own beginnings with you, Rosalind, and incubated them over all these years. We used to talk in metaphors. You told me about the cleaver and the talking bells and how Angelo from Italy was waiting inside you to be born again. But he was dead, you said, and you felt a sense of failure. And you told me of your dreams and fears. You could play with words like a juggler at a fair.

I wish I had been able to see that you were ill, that what had begun as your usual scattiness had turned into an appeal, that your metaphors had become suddenly real. Even the paranoia was always there, you used to say that it ran in the blood. If a plant died in your Uncle Jeremy's greenhouse, he would look around for footprints in the mud to see if 'Bolshie elements' from the village had been in and poisoned it. The village was a three-mile walk away. Your mother was paranoid. And you were paranoid. How I wish I had known that you were behind those barricades at Larenguebec, hiding in a dark cupboard in the attic. But it didn't occur to me that you could be there.

So I went back down the hill to the beach, I wasn't looking for a sick lady fighting to survive. I didn't know that you were up there hiding from the heat and the crabs and the flies and from the people who seemed to hate you, and the bells in your head that would not leave you, and from the ectoplasm of your guilt feelings, and from the Centrale that was trying to destroy you with its leaking radiation. I was looking for the old you I remembered, not the shadow and the scourge locked in their battle. That was why I went down on to the beach to surprise you lying in the sun, tired by the children and needing me to take you home; or just playing roly-poly in the sand with Amadeo and wanting me to join in the fun.

I followed the steep path down into the scant village. To my right, there was a sharp drop and then the beach. To my left, some twenty stone cottages straddled the road edge. It was almost impossible to tell if they were inhabited or not, such was their air of decay. Clumps of dead nettles were rooted under the slabs of limestone that served as roofs, and peeling paintwork flaked on to the walls. I remember feeling embarrassed at being so 'English' in my reactions to the village itself. My first feeling was that the decay was unhealthy and the silence sinister. I even found the stares of the bleary-eyed men who were sitting at the edge of the road, staring out towards the massive steel drums of the Centrale, sinister. It was too hot to think anything for long, though. I chided myself, mentally, and walked on: why should peasants smile, and why should they fit my identikit picture of 'the locals'.

At the bottom of the hill there was a shop with a bar behind it. Outside were two plastic bubble-gum machines. Inside, four men were playing cards; they ignored me. The barmaid had a sour, bitter face, and she, too, tried to ignore me. I ordered a cognac, and drank it. I asked her about you, and the deep lines around her mouth tightened slightly. When I asked her again, she shrugged and held her nose and leered across at one of the men playing cards, who smiled back at her knowingly. As I asked a third time, she turned her back on me.

The cognac went straight to my head and I felt myself stagger as I left the bar. On one side of a stone lighthouse rampart there was the abandoned harbour and a mass of rocks and stones. Barely visible beyond a beach were the monstrous cylinders of the nuclear plant. On the other side of the harbour, there was a stretch of sand and boulders curving away for mile upon mile, lined by two cliffs and fields. It was a magnificent view, the sort of view that could make you dreamy for hours, Rosalind. I couldn't see you anywhere along the beach, but I felt that you would be out that way. After twenty minutes of trekking over the hot sand, I began to wonder how you could have stumbled any further with the pram and the circus of girls and the picnic that you would inevitably have brought. I was already too hot to bother, and I sat down to rest. I think I sat and stared at the bare cuttle-fish bones and the crabs' claws, the circling gulls and at the sea itself. Then I buried my face in my bag and fell asleep.

IX

William

I woke up, hours later, feeling sick and dizzy from the sun. I scanned the littered shore for you, but the beach was deserted. I felt suddenly angry. I wanted to see you, and I resented your apparent disappearance. How could so many of you disappear as though into the fourth dimension in a village the size of Larenguebec? I felt manipulated by circumstances, trapped, almost in the swing doors of fate, to turn and turn and miss my every chance. I imagined you all traipsing back from your picnic and passing wide of the man in the sand that was me sleeping. On my way back to the harbour, I vented my wrath on the stray bladderwrack, bursting the drying sacks of brine. I walked back along the cool edge of the receding tide, looking among the newly washed shingle for bits of coloured glass for you and shells for the twins. Instead, I found only little piles of dismembered crabs' limbs quilted in flies' wings. I passed the bar again and the lighthouse wall and walked on across the rocks and stones in the opposite direction towards the distant Centrale. It seemed perverse of you to have come there, and I was unconsciously gathering bits of crab, and consciously thinking bad things about you, when I saw the pram.

It was standing on its own, as lifeless in its way as the lighthouse, but I didn't see that at first. It had what appeared to be a new dark sunshade, and between me and it, the twins were digging in the sand. As I approached them they looked up once, but made no sign of recognition. They were burnt the colour of Baltic pine, and their hair looked irrevocably tangled. They seemed so intent on shovelling their sand that I thought they were purposely ignoring me. They were in their turquoise swimming costumes – both knitted by Mrs King to some pre-war pattern that she had unearthed – and they managed somehow to look both savage and vulnerable. I felt an urge to pick them up and hold them, and brush out their hair, and clear away the frowns that seemed to be binding them to the sand. I knew, though, that they would resent any demonstration of affection in public – not that the beach at Larenguebec was very public. Even when I stood right beside them, they kept shovelling, maniacally, heaping up the slipping sand into a long mound.

'Aren't you going to say hello?' I asked.

'We're burying crabs.'

'Where's Mummy?'

'She's back at the house, she doesn't come out any more.'

There was a strange smell of old crab meat, of beach debris, of shells and fish and rotting flesh in the sun, and then an undertow of something else. It mixed in with the heat and made me feel physically sick. The twins' games were often perverse. They collected dead things wherever they went. I felt suddenly annoyed with them for this penchant for gathering slime and rubbish. They should have known better than to pollute their brothers' pram, and they had no business to be out on their own. I approached them as any father might approach his children. I wasn't looking for trouble, I was looking for my family: a special, but still a normal, family on holiday. I assumed that Amadeo was with you, or walking with Candy.

I looked down at the toy shovels that the twins held in their hands; but for their size, they could've been workmen's tools, worn and stunted with heavy use. Then I saw their hands were calloused and blistered, their fingers slightly swollen where they tightened around the wooden handles of the spades. I saw, too, that the vulnerability that had so moved me before had taken the form of a tiredness in them. I recalled newsreels of men working in labour camps carrying stones from a quarry; those men had had the same desperate fatigue in their faces that my children had. I looked up and across at the pram, and they winced. I felt that they needed taking in hand.

'Come on,' I said, touching their hot shoulders to guide them with me. They seemed relieved to stop digging but instead of following me, they trod down the sand they had just turned.

'Come on,' I called again, firmly, from a pace or two away from them. They didn't follow me, so I went back and with an arm around each of them we walked on. Halfway to the pram they stopped abruptly, shook out their woolly swimming things, and then squared themselves to dig again. Together they marked out a rectangle some three feet by one.

'Still burying crabs?'

'Yup.'

'Why?'

'They've eaten Candy,' one of them told me, then the other one interrupted, 'Well she fell in the sea, actually.'

'. . . and then they ate her!'

'They did not.'

'Did.'

They had stopped digging now and were poised to fight, with their small fists trembling to be right.

'When did Candy fall into the sea?' I asked patiently. They spoke half to me, and half to each other.

'After she fell they ate her,' one said stubbornly.

'You know she went away. We know that.'

But the other didn't want to hear or know, and the tears were smarting in her eyes.

'Candy was like our family, she wouldn't just go. The crabs are eating our family. We have to bury the crabs.' I looked from one to the other, from the set look of one to the quivering lip of the other. They were both scared of something, and I felt scared for them, and sorry to see this first rift in their partnership.

'When did Candy go?' I asked again.

They both paused, and a sudden wave of boredom registered on their identical faces.

'Oh, ages ago,' they answered in unison.

That was when I knew that something really bad had happened. They lived in their own world most of the time, where fantasy and lies merged into one indistinguishable mesh. They never grew tired of their games; so if they were bored, it was with something real. I wanted to think clearly, but the smell of the beach and the debris was smothering me.

There was violence in the air at Larenguebec. I felt myself in the grip of alien emotions. I felt angry again, perhaps for the third or fourth time that day. I wasn't used to feeling like that. I looked out across the littered sand and cursed the place that had nothing for me but bad feelings. With what energy I had left, I wanted to gather the twins and the pram and get back to you and Amadeo and take you all away from that crustacean cemetery. As we approached the pram, I could see that the new canopy was a haze of living flies, and the interior of the pram was heaped with decaying crabs. For once, I was really angry with the twins. They were using the pram as a sea hearse. As we approached it, the twins dropped behind, though I scarcely noticed at the time. The strange, chemical smell seemed to be coming downwind from the Centrale, but a worse smell was now coming from the pram itself. I couldn't get to it without my handkerchief over my face. I took hold of the porcelain bar on the handle with its thin line of gold and its trademark painted and worn away by your hands. I pushed it blindly through the cloud of hovering flies, struggling to force its wheels through the dry sand. The twins were calling now, but their voices were as unintelligible as the gulls to me. Then one of them was tugging at my shirt.

'Daddy, don't go that way, Daddy, that's the Centrale, it's bad, it's where the smell comes from.'

I stumbled forward with the pram for a few more yards, but it was sinking in its tracks. The twins were whimpering now. They never whimpered. When I ignored them, they ran round in front of the pram and stood blocking the path.

'Don't you understand? It's evil. It'll kill you, like it's doing to Mummy and Amadeo!'

I didn't know what they were talking about, but I began to share their fear. One half of me wanted them to speak again, the other half dreaded it. Then it came.

'Mummy says that she has to stay in, and Amadeo has to go out . . . to get better.'

'It's the sickness,' the other one of them explained to me gently, touching my hand to ease the blow.

I wanted to ask them where Amadeo was, and sensed that they heard me telepathically, but hadn't the strength to reply. Watching them broke the spell of the Centrale, which had somehow been drawing me into its field. Now, one twin still stood defiantly blocking my path, while the other had let go of my hand and was moving slowly back to join her sister. Their faces had grown pale under their tans and it seemed that they were set as with plaster of Paris.

I began to lift the bits of crap out of the pram. The flies went berserk. I could hardly breathe, but I kept on tipping the claws and shells and heads on to the sand. My head was turned away. The twins had moved back instinctively, and I knew from the horror on their faces that I would find Amadeo in the pram. His hair was bleached almost white, and his face bore the same deep tan as the girls, but his lips were cracked and his face was parched and peeling. The frills of his lace shirt looked more like layers of a soiled dressing. He lay completely dull and listless, incarcerated by the abominable smell. I stroked his warm forehead, but his huge grey eyes didn't move from the point on the side of the pram that he was staring at. I held by breath and leant over and whispered to him, but I was answered only by flies.

'How could you?' I asked. But the twins stared blankly at the sea.

'How long as he been in there?' I asked.

'Oh, ages.'

'Jesus!'

Now the twins stopped, hands on hips, and suddenly annoyed by my apparent stupidity.

'He can't hold up his head. We went to the Centrale, and now he's got the sickness, and so has Mummy. She says she has to stay in the dark, and Amadeo has to stay in the sun.'

'Why?'

'Because of the smell, of course. But you mustn't take him near the Centrale, or she'll be furious.'

I tried to lift Amadeo out, but he whimpered when I touched him, and I didn't dare move him more. It was the first sound he had made since I found him. I could hardly move, my joints were so stiff with foreboding, but his sigh gave me the courage to turn the pram and set back in the opposite direction, towards the village and the house again, and you, Rosalind.

'Why didn't Candy call a doctor?'

'Candy was scared, she just left.'

'She did not, she fell in the sea.'

'She's a cow, she saw that Amadeo woke up dead, she saw it and she saw he was all right before, and she saw he woke up dead and she just left us.' The twins were pulling at each other's swimming things now, tugging at the turquoise wool and stretching it, ready to tear and fight, but again, one of them was tearful.

'She didn't, she wouldn't, she fell in the sea.'

We reached the slope of the hill and I pushed the pram harder now, labouring under the still hot sun. The villagers were there, staring. I noticed that the four who had been in the bar playing cards were now out on the street too, frowning and muttering. Someone spat as the twins passed, and the gobbet fell a few inches away from their sandalled feet.

'Why do they hate us like this?'

The twins didn't seem to mind. I envied them their ability to escape from their surroundings as I watched them trudging up the hill with their spades and their blisters and their tangled hair: just two eight-year-old children on holiday in France.

'There isn't a doctor here,' one of them said. Then the other piped up, in answer to my previous question.

'I suppose because of the smell, they hate most things.'

'Like what?'

'Like the Centrale, and Candy, and the others.'

We walked on again under the stares and the heat.

'Mummy needs a doctor,' one of them volunteered. Then together they added.

'That's why we called you.'

I kept pushing, and they kept walking, swinging their spades.

'There isn't a doctor here.'

At the shop, the twins wanted things. They wanted gobstoppers and bubble gum from the slot machines outside, and they wanted new spades to bury more crabs, and they wanted horsemeat for the cat. I didn't dare go into that shop, it was all I could do to walk past the villagers, shoving that foul stench of the pram up the hill, and watching them exchange looks as we passed. The twins relinquished their claims on the gobstoppers, and walked ahead of me, apparently unconcerned by the fuss. As we neared the crossroads I felt myself leaning more and more heavily on the pram as my knees weakened. A fat slow-eyed boy was leaning against a wall, he looked about sixteen and very sweaty. As the twins passed him, he lunged forward, trying to grab the nearest on her flat sunburnt chest. As he reached out, he leered at me with an unpleasant complicity. I didn't see what happened next, but the boy pulled back his hand bleeding from a deep gash.

'*Putains*,' he said, and turned back to the wall, clutching his wound. The twins were proud of themselves, and they showed me the sharpened cuttle-fish bones they were holding in their hands.

'They're not going to touch us.'

'Not after what they did to Candy.'

'What did they do to Candy?' I asked, despite myself, breaking my earlier silence.

'Well they're not going to do it to us,' they said firmly, and then continued up the hill, swinging their worn spades.

I had never really liked Candy, but I still wondered what had happened to her; what had she done in this god-forsaken place? The taxi-driver was right, this was no place for the likes of any of us. I even wondered if they might have pushed her into the sea, but I didn't think so. The twins lied a lot, they often lied, but one of them wasn't lying today, and the other one was just frightened. I couldn't think much about Candy though. She had never been much use, it didn't surprise me that she had been useless here in France as well. I coudln't care, somehow, about her, I had to care about Amadeo, and keeping the flies off him, and getting back, and making him well, and somehow making my ancient twins eight again, and most of all, I had to find you.

When we reached the house, a drunkard was sitting propped up by the road, fondling his dog.

'That's Pierre,' one of the twins whispered, then, 'Hello Pierre.'

He stared at her, looking somewhere halfway between her and her double, looking confused, probably seeing four girls instead of two. He turned his head away without replying.

'He never talks,' they explained.

The door was still locked when I tried it, but the twins had gone on past the house, beckoning me round after them. I pushed on up a dirt track, feeling that at any moment the pram would run back over me. Once in the back garden, there was a tiny flight of stairs to negotiate, then a footbridge, then a door.

'What about Amadeo?'

'Oh, we always leave him here, you can't get it down the steps, it'd tip.'

There was a view out over rooftops and the bay, curving slowly round to the tip of Normandy. The grass and weeds were knee deep and scorched by the long summer. I tried to lift poor 'Deo out again then, but his clothes were stuck to the mattress. The smell when I moved it was more than I could bear, and I gagged.

'You do go on about it,' one of them moaned. 'We've been living with it for weeks.'

I straightened myself and turned back to lift again.

'Mummy thinks he's still alive, too. She sends him out into the sun to get better. She goes spare when I try to tell her how long it's been.'

'But he sighed,' I said, 'he whimpered.'

They both came to me now, and we held hands above the nettles. One was silent, and one spoke.

'It's because of the flies. We want to bury him, but we don't dare. Mummy thinks it's her sickness that makes her see 'Deo like this. So we bury the crabs instead, and then, those people can't put their eyes on him, they've all got the sickness, I think . . . Candy was a cow, she saw he woke up dead.'

The silent twin had let go of my hand, and slumped down on to the top step. I noticed that a briar rose and a sweet pea grew incongruously out of the wilderness of nettles that lined the descent.

X

Rosalind

Sometimes I can remember it was dark in the attic. I needed the dark. I don't like to remember. Sometimes the morning came and tried to steal my dark. Hathers says mornings are for jigsaws. Mornings are jigsaws. My children are pieces. I can't find the right place for them. I know where they go, but I can't find the right way round. Hathers takes hours with puzzles; I can usually find the pieces quickly and put them in for her. Sometimes she likes to put them in herself, and then I just put them near. She hasn't come today, not for a long time. If she knew how threatened my dark was, I think she'd come. She never knew I used to hide. I didn't tell her. If I had told her that Uncle Bertie and I were hiding, it would probably have been all right. If she knew, she would come. She would come now into my cracks of light and pull the curtains over them. If it wasn't for always my fault, she would come.

When we first arrived here, I was frightened. The people seemed to want to scoop my brain out with their stares. I saw the crab shells on the road, and I thought, 'They want to scoop out my skull like that.' And they kept spitting. I needed to get away. We were too near to my troubles in Tanza Road. I could even hear the bells sometimes, and I was getting sad about Amadeo. I tried to explain it to William, and I think he understood, but it didn't help me inside, because I didn't need understanding, I needed my baby back. Women feel like that, I think, when a child is stillborn. William thought that I wanted to get away from him, but I didn't. When we were at home I used to wander off. I went to the Royal Free Hospital once and asked a girl in the Administration what they did with the stillborn babies. I pretended that my sister had given birth to one there two years before, when my Amadeo was born. I said she wanted to know where it would have been buried. She found out for me, and told me about the mound in Highgate Cemetery where the nameless children go. I used to go there too. I used to try and concentrate very hard to find out by the feel which part of the mound could have my own dead baby buried under it. I wanted to ask William to help me. But I knew he would just insist that the baby didn't die, but was Amadeo. Then I would tell him there were two Amadeos: my newborn one who died because I wouldn't let him come; and the one who lived with us. Identical twins, like the girls, but boys and in the image of Angelo.

People think that if they mention a dead person it will remind you and make you sad. They think that if they mention my stillborn child, it will be bad for me. But I need to hear about him. I need to hear his name, to see his grave, to work out my grief. I told William that. I explained that for me there had to be two Amadeos. After that, he would sometimes talk about them both, but he never did so naturally. In some countries, people have special rites for mourning, and they accept death much more easily than we do. Maybe if there had been a wake and a proper funeral, then I wouldn't have felt so guilty about my lost baby. I don't know, though: you have to feel guilty when you do something wrong. After the Amadeos were born, when I came out of hospital, I went to confession. I wanted to atone for the lost one. Father Harrison told me to rest. The next week I went again, but in the meantime he must have been talking to people, for he began to cover things up, to pretend that nothing had happened. He talked a lot of rubbish to me. He wouldn't listen. How can I rest with all this guilt? How can I rest if I can't even confess it?

Things were coming to disturb me. I thought that if I got away, somewhere near the sea, they would go away. I didn't realize about the Centrale. Everywhere I go to hide is bad. This time, I went to hide in a place stricken by radiation sickness. All the locals had it. I could see they were strange from the first day. When I closed my eyes the bells tried to deafen me. When I opened them, Angelo was there. Angelo and Amadeo had the same eyes, the same curls, the same waxen beauty. Angelo was carrying my stillborn baby in his arms, carrying it as the doctors had from the foot of my bed. Only the sight of Amadeo playing in the sun could make the vision go away. He loves the sun. I love the twilight and the dark, but he loves the sun.

So I would come out into the daylight with Candy and the girls, and walk through the gauntlet of stares in the village. And we'd go on to the beach with our picnic and our wine and the toys, and he'd be so happy, he'd laugh and roll on the sand. Then I'd feel strong enough to pass through each bad day to the next one, and something tried to unwind in me. Candy was frightening the twins, telling them things she picked up from the villagers about the Centrale. I felt that Candy was out of her depth. I warned her not to flirt. She told me that I was jealous of her. She was going out with a Guernseyman who had been washed ashore in his boat. He had to wait for a tide. He was superstitious and told her things about the Centrale. Some days, when the sun caught on the cylinders and flashed across the beach, I too felt odd about the Centrale, but I didn't want the twins to be afraid. We always went to the long beach and the sand and the cliffs. One day, though, I took them the other way, to the sands in front of the Centrale. I wanted to show them that they were safe with me.

We had a lovely day. It was Sunday, I remember. I realize now that I should have known better on a Sunday, but I didn't think of it then. A van was selling roast lamb on a spit parked outside the bar, and we bought a lot of hot meat and fresh bread and apple juice and wine. We played *boules* on the sand. Amadeo played too, and got quite good at rolling the coloured wooden balls. He could always hit the yellow ones. That was because he liked the sun. It was the first day that the twins seemed properly relaxed. Amadeo used to get sleepy after lunch. Usually I would wheel him back at that point, and sit in the dark with him while he had his daily rest. That day I turned him away from the sun. I know now that I shouldn't have turned him towards the Centrale. I thought it would shade him, but it just made him ill.

That night, Angelo came into the attic and sat with me. He arrived carrying my stillborn baby. He had dressed it in one of Amadeo's gowns, which was much too big for it. He gave me the dead baby, but I knew that I mustn't take it, because if I did it would hurt my live Amadeo. When I tried to give it back to him, he turned into the bells and the bells were talking again. In the morning, he gave the baby to Candy. It was like a big doll. It had Amadeo's eyes. Candy tried to give it to me too, but I knew that I still mustn't take it. I don't know where Candy went. I think the tide changed and she sailed away with the Guernseyman. Some of the villagers had made her cry before. I'd warned her. The twins kept coming and going. They didn't seem to have so many games without Candy. They kept pestering me. Sometimes they brought the stillborn baby back to me. They kept asking me to bury it again. I've been to the place in Highgate where the dead babies go. I've stood on the mound. I can't join in all their games. They have games that are part of their world, and they don't understand about the two Amadeos. I don't think they ever knew about the other baby. Nobody seems to know about it except William and me. It's very strange.

Hathers used to ask me things. When we went to see *Dick Whittington*, she never understood how bells could talk. I thought that she was silly then. Now I know how hard it is to make people grasp things.

It was dark in the attic. I needed the dark. I had to cry when the light came through the door. And I had to cry whenever the twins came, because they were my children, and real, and somewhere I had dream children who were lost. I still cry sometimes when I lose things. There was no television in Larenguebec, there were no films.

After Amadeo was born and died so nearly stillborn that I call him that, I couldn't bear the guilt for my lost child, so I pretended that he was alive still, and growing, and sometimes they humoured me. William was good to me. Maybe I could have had a more conventional grief in another country. Maybe in Ireland, or on the Mediterranean, they would have known how to take my child from me without breaking my heart; or maybe it can't be done. Then I lived inside a dark cushion for two years. I was tormented by my guilt because if the birth had been quicker, if I had pushed when they told me, if I hadn't hidden him so long inside me, he might have had the strength to live.

Well, in Larenguebec, I felt as if I was going mad. I really thought I was. I even thought that William was against me. He tried to show me the baby in the gown, but I didn't let him. The bells screamed in my head and I screamed them out to him and they went away. They all went away, and the next day we went to Switzerland. William wanted me to go into a clinic, a nuthouse. I didn't want to, but I thought 'I'm better now, and he's humoured me for two years, so I'll humour him for a few weeks.' I liked the clinic actually. I had a television in my room and a video machine and there were lovely gardens. I can't remember how long I stayed there, I suppose it was about a month. Some of the doctors were a bit much, but, on the whole, they were all right. There was one in particular who kept talking about my career. I suppose there are actresses who like discussing their films, but, frankly, I don't. I'd rather talk about anything else under the sun. Anything, that is, except perhaps the Amadeos. There was another doctor there, a German, who was obsessed by them. I did my best with him, but he was hopeless.

When we went back to London, William and I were very close again. He seemed sad, though; as I had been before. They had asked me at the clinic about the grave in Highgate. There wasn't much they didn't ask me. I felt like telling them that I was getting my money's worth just with the gardens and the video machine, and I was quite well and they didn't need to delve into my psyche quite so vigorously. But I suppose they had their job to do, and they couldn't know I was only with them to humour Willie. Just about everything I told them got back to Willie. It would have been much simpler to have had him pull up a chair and listen in: I didn't tell them anything that I didn't want him to hear.

So when we went back to South End Green, William asked me to take him to the grave. It's a plain communal grave. I don't like the thought of mass graves. It seems inappropriate unless there's a war or an epidemic. I showed him the mound, and we went a couple of times more together. Poor old Willie, he seems really scared sometimes. I honestly think he's afraid of Mrs King.

I always wanted the twins to go away to school. I used to try and explain to William about my own childhood; how I never went to school, and how I missed it, and how I had felt unprotected. He hated the idea of a boarding school. He told me about his school and the dreadful time that he'd spent there. He would tell me such cruel stories about it that I would be convinced for a month or so, and then I'd start pestering him again. It's different for girls. Girls have to be protected, it's not enough just to mean well. Nobody could have been better intentioned than Hathers, but she couldn't protect me. Also, the twins were so clever and so wild, I'd get frightened for them. The twins themselves always seemed to like the idea of boarding school. I expect that was partly because I had been suggesting to them what a wonderful time and what amazing facilities they would have there. They knew that Willie didn't enjoy 'school talk'. I think his own memories were still too raw. But whenever I could persuade him, we would discuss the pros and cons of all the potential establishments. Over the years, we had filled in the forms, paid the registration fees and put down the twins' names for most of the big ones, some of the small ones, and even one or two abroad.

I wouldn't ever have forced the issue of the twins' school if William had remained against it, but I was pleased when he decided to send them. They seemed to start with almost indecent haste. There weren't many schools that we'd all agreed on. Usually, I liked one and they liked another, and we would rummage through the brochures. By the time they were eight, there was a place in Gloucestershire, two on the south coast, one in Scotland and a couple of others. As it happened there was also one in Switzerland, just outside Lausanne, which we'd all liked, but which had always seemed 'a bit too far'. This school, besides being on the edge of Lake Léman, had a private zoo with otters and chimpanzees and wombats. The twins had an obsession with wombats. Perhaps William thought somewhere abroad would be less likely to resemble his own old school – I don't know.

We had a flat in the clinic. Or rather, I had my room in the main block, and they had a flat in a chalet in the grounds. After William had taken them to see the school, the twins were so excited, they would talk of nothing else. They came back with the boot of the hired car heaped up with new and second-hand clothes from the school shop, and we spent the next two days ironing on name tapes and inking them in. I wanted to wait until we could get proper tapes with their names embroidered on, like the ones my cousins used to have. But they were all too impatient.

Once, when these cousins of mine came for Christmas, when I was about nine, I was tremendously impressed by all their name tags. Even their vests and socks had blue and white tapes with George, and Edmund, Palliser embroidered on them. At the time, I had visions of dozens of figures, more agile than Hathers, handsewing these names, and I remarked to my Uncle Bertie what a tremendous labour it must be. I could hardly believe him when he told me that it was done in six weeks. Why six weeks? For years after, it seemed like a magical length of time. My village was a long way from the world of mail orders and sewing machines that knew how to embroider. Six weeks later, a fat letter arrived for me and was carried up to the nursery floor, opened by Hathers and then passed to me. I nearly died of excitement. I had six dozen name tapes, each with my own 'Rosalind' in red italics, an 'F' for Florence and a 'V' for Vivienne and then my surname on a long bordered strip of white cotton. That was the nicest present I've ever had. I didn't have six dozen things to put them on, but Hathers and I stitched them to my handkerchiefs and teddy bears and face flannels, and I even stuck one around my thimble with Sellotape. There was a receipt in Bertie's name with the tapes, and nothing else. They made me feel famous. They came from Nottingham. I'd never been to Nottingham, but now, all over the Midlands, people had been stitching my name. I felt that there must be hundreds of seamstresses wondering what the 'F' and the 'V' stood for. I was almost tempted to publish a notice in the local newspaper that the 'V' was for my mother, and the 'F' was a family name that all the Pallisers girls had. When I became famous in the cinema, it never brought such a flush of pride to my cheeks as that packet of cotton strips bearing my name. I know now that they are machine made, but someone still had to work the machine, take the order, check the stitches.

I could tell that the twins felt proud, even with their iron-on tapes and their indelible laundry markers. It was strange to divide their identity into two sets of clothes, two sets of pencils. They had always had a common pool. I don't know if they ever really thought of themselves as two people, with different names. I wrote the two names out for them, but when it came to dividing up the uniform and the home clothes, they seemed unable to agree on who was Florence and who was Harriet.

I suggested that they decided by their lockets. Even that failed to settle the dispute. In fact, it exacerbated it. The one with the 'Harriet' on her locket claimed that she had only swapped it the week before.

They were holding each other's sleeves again, which was often their way of fighting. They would just stand stubbornly, sometimes for hours, each holding the other's sleeves at the elbow, and staring into the other's eyes. I had seen so many of these battles of will that I decided to arbitrate before they became exhausted.

'Why don't you each make a list of all the times you've swapped lockets, and whoever remembers the most can choose her name?' It had a magical effect. It never mattered how good my suggestion might be; any outside intervention invariably drew them together again. Now, moving in perfect unison, they dropped elbows, relaxed and presented their usual united front, speaking together, unrehearsed, in the way that disconcerted so many people.

'We don't mind who is who, you choose.'

It was always my wish, my decision, to send them to school, but as the week drew to a close and they prepared to leave, I wanted to keep them back. They seemed so eager to go, and to be with other children. They had never shown any desire to play with their peers before, but they seemed somehow to have regressed, to want to be young, to be eight, to play normal games. It was as though they had buried their precocity at Larenguebec.

I realized now how unwell I must have been at Larenguebec when I saw the state of their hands. They had blisters all over the palms, and calluses along the edges. Even when they started school, there were still some raw patches, despite the salves and the bandages I had used all week. They had always liked digging. They used to dig at Tanza Road. They had a kind of pit behind the shrubbery, and they would dig there for hours and hours, unearthing worms and ants and centipedes, and, on wet days, gathering slugs. They had a passion for collecting animals, hence their keenness on the school with the zoo. Of course, zoos try to collect their animals alive and keep them that way, which was something that the twins found hard to understand. But they always liked digging.

Once, my mother came to visit, when they were about four, and she was struck by the depth of their pit. She said, 'My goodness, they're digging so hard, they'll soon be unearthing your Uncle Bertie in Australia.' Then she looked at me, and blushed a little, and went inside. It was the first time that she had mentioned Bertie since I was a child in unspoken disgrace. It had a strange effect on me. The twins were still not talking then, and they didn't say a thing for another two years. When they were little, they often gave no impression of hearing or understanding what was said to them, but in this case, they did.

We went to Brancaster after your father died. I didn't go to the funeral. I went to the beach instead with the girls. I suppose I should have gone, but I couldn't face that bleak rectory even for a few hours. On the other hand, I didn't want you to have the slow journey alone, and then be thrown back into the church and the graveyard, following your dead father in hushed obligatory respect, as he had always made you do in his lifetime. So I went to Brancaster, which was nearby and had a small hotel, and a beach for the twins, while you went to the funeral. I was pregnant, I remember, with Amadeo, and it was very hot. I sat on a towel on the sand and read a book, while the twins dug a hole beside me. They had begun to talk not long before, and it was a pleasure just to hear their voices after so many years of silence from them.

I asked, 'What are you digging?' and they said, together, as they always did.

'We're digging a pit for you to go down to your Uncle Bertie in Australia.'

XI

William

I never imagined that Amadeo was dead. Even when I saw him staring out from under the crabs in the pram on the beach, I never thought that he wasn't alive. He didn't look ill, or wounded, he looked sunburnt. He was hot to touch. When I first saw him there, I was shocked, and then I was angry. The twins were treating him like a doll. I knew that a baby with a fever can look very still, but I touched him, and he moved, and I know that he made a sound. I suppose it was just the sounds that neglected corpses make. By rights, he should have changed: it was as though something had overruled the natural course of nature, and preserved his uncanny beauty. Maybe it was the hot sand that the twins had banked him up in, the salt from the crabs, or just some strange phenomenon beyond my comrephension, but he looked alive. Even later that night when I buried him, he looked alive.

I think I mean, though, that he didn't look dead. There was nothing unpleasant about the sight of him, except for the peeling of his skin and his stained clothes. All the time that I wheeled him across the beach, and then back to the house, I was angry that my son, or anybody's son, should be heaped up with crabs. There was an indecency about it; and Amadeo had always been so scrupulously clean where smells were concerned. He thought nothing of lining the entire inner surface of a house with jam or chocolate, but he could never abide bad smells. He was sensitive too. The twins would pick up dead pigeons from the street and carry them home to keep for as long as they could get away with it. But Amadeo would weep for dead things on the kerb, and wanted to revive all the heaps

102

of feathers that his sisters kept stored under their beds. He even used to plead for the lives of snails when the twins began their garden witch-hunts, armed with sticks and tin cans. So, of all people, why was he covered over with the decomposed flotsam?

I could see that the twins were sorry. I didn't realize at the time, though, that they were sorry for you and the baby, and not for any misdemeanour of their own. They had been given a burden that no one should have to carry, let alone an eight-year-old child. When you were at the height of your sickness, hallucinating in the dark, cut off from reason, they not only took the baby away, they protected you, Rosalind, instinctively. They covered Amadeo with crabs so that no one should blame you, their mother, who was ill and could not bear any blame or hostile intervention. They found you screaming in the attic, rejecting what should have been your shared grief, and they protected you. Day after day they covered up your madness. Day after day they wheeled their brother into the sun as your schizophrenia ordered them to. They could have hidden him in the garden, but you insisted that he go out on to the sand, into the sun, and they took him, sensing the dangers of discovery; they took him to be loyal to you.

You were always right, Rosalind, whatever you did was right. Even with the evidence to the contrary under their eyes, you were still right for them. Now that you have converted our son into a figment of your imagination and buried him in Highgate Cemetery in your mind, they have too. You say he never lived, and they never say he died. You say he was stillborn, and they accept that version of your motherhood. Parents have a terrible power over a child – they can create the world or destroy it.

All the days when the twins were burying crabs, I think they were burying their own uneasiness. They dug pits in the sand. They took the crabs off Amadeo and buried them, then replaced them with new ones, and by this ritual they buried their dead brother. Yet every night, they wheeled him home to you, and every morning you sent them out again. Then the pattern was repeated, and the blisters formed on their hands as they worked longer and longer hours scouring the beach for crustaceans.

A sudden death doesn't have any real impact at the time it occurs. Once the first wave of shock passes, the brain seems to slow down and accelerate in strange ways, and a numb drifting sets in with just occasional irrational thoughts bursting through. When I went to lift Amadeo out of his pram in the back garden at Larenguebec, I found that he was stiff and hard. The twins told me he was dead. I thought he was a doll. A heavy, waxen doll that someone had put in his place. I felt suddenly relieved. It had been disconcerting to find him sunk in squalor on the beach. Now I seemed to understand. This was not my son, this was an effigy that the twins had found. I marvelled that an effigy from such a remote part of Normandy could be so like our Amadeo; then I remembered Angelo standing on the water. They both had grey eyes, and you had grey eyes. I wanted to see you. I moved to put the baby down, the wax thing in his clothes, and then another wave hit me with a new breath and the appalling smell. One part of me knew that it was Amadeo, the real one, and one part of me denied it; but even my bones knew that something was terribly wrong.

He was like a doll to carry, with his unbending limbs and his head lying stiffly on his neck. I carried him with me into the house. I remember wondering if I should leave him outside as the twins had suggested, but my urge to protect him, even though it was too late, was stronger than my reason. He was unnaturally heavy, and I stumbled on the stairs. We didn't speak, the twins and I. They knew that I wanted you, and they led me up into the attic and then they stood back and let me pass by them into the smothering darkness of your hiding place.

It was hot up there, in the low attic room under the bare rafters. I was reminded of the drying-room at the rectory, the only warm room in the house with its cupboard-like dimensions and the hot-water tank radiating heat. The three dormer windows in the roof at Larenguebec were boarded over, and the only light came through cracks in the wood and tiles. There were discarded and broken pieces of furniture heaped up between crates, piles of newspapers and old tins of paint. It was as though a whole generation of dust had gathered there and never been disturbed. I felt my way through that long attic room to a doorway at one end. I don't know why I thought that you would be in the end room. I think I just wanted you not to be in the desiccated squalor of the long attic, and I hoped, even after all the events of the afternoon, I hoped that you would be safe somewhere, and all right.

Going to Larenguebec was like having a glove stretcher forced into my credulity. Each time I took a step, it seemed, I had to redefine the worst I could expect. I edged my way through the dim light to the darkness of your room, from the crumbling familiarity of disused furniture to the surreal hothouse of your insanity. When I went in, at first, I couldn't see you. It was too dark. I opened the dividing door, and you screamed.

I had never heard you scream before in real life. Once, on the screen, in a film, you had had to scream, and you did so with such piercing conviction that it earned an '18' rating at the cinema. Then, the twins could scream in such a way that it made me want to weep and run away. I used to think that they would break windows and shatter glass like the singer in my Tin Tin books. It was your scream. They always knew things before I did. They must have sensed this cry of yours and copied it.

When I went into your room at Larenguebec, you screamed so loud that I thought you would damage your throat. I couldn't see what condition you were in, but I was afraid. All afternoon I had been wading through calamity. Yet somehow I managed to keep some vestige of my natural optimism. When I reached your darkness, though, it was like the end of the road, the end of my hope, and I feared for your life. I moved instinctively towards you, wanting to see the worst quickly, to face whatever horror there was and get it over with. I tripped on something, then steadied myself. I was still carrying Amadeo, outstretched and rigid in my arms. I stumbled back then, into the half-light of the long ante-room, and I laid him down on a pile of old sacking. For all the long seconds that I struggled to find a place to lay him in, to get my balance and return to you, your voice threatened to break down the house, burst my head, destroy us all.

Then I went back in, alone, into that den of dead air, and you were suddenly quiet. I stood in the miraculous hush and tried to focus my eyes. I heard you say 'William', and I turned my head in the direction of your voice. That was almost the end of the bad time. Other things were still very wrong, but they were never like that again. Through the dim light that came from the doorway behind me, I saw you sitting in the corner on the floor, on a kind of makeshift raft of rags and bundles of toys.

There seemed to be a long silence after that. I wanted to say something but I didn't know what, and every time I tried just to talk and let whatever words would come be spoken, my tongue seemed to grow dry and heavy. I could see you staring at me, and I was aware of staring back. It was like the day that we saw Angleo. You looked at him then as though he were your salvation, or maybe just the embodiment of your dreams. So we stared, motionless, until the voice of the twins broke the spell.

'We're going to play in the garden.'

I can't remember what either of us said. I don't think I said much at all, but you talked. A lot of words seemed to tumble out of you. They didn't all make sense. Sometimes they merged into a big jumble and then you said clean, coherent things like,

'I've been very ill, Willie, thank God I'm better now.'

I know I asked you over and over, 'What happened?'

You still haven't answered that one. But when I asked too often, you started to cry. Then you stopped and beckoned me into your corner of toys and ribboned gowns. I sat down beside you, and held you to me. The touch of you made me cry; it began as silent tears welling in my eyes and rolling down my face. I had learnt to cry like that, silently, so that I could hide and not be found by my mother or father or by any of their parishioners. Later on, at school, it stood me in good stead to be able to lie in my metal bed and weep under the privacy of my top sheet and not let any of the other boys detect so much as a murmur or a tremble. Nothing much made me want to cry after I grew up. I didn't cry when mother died, though I did feel uncontrollably vulnerable for the best part of a year. Then, when we were engaged, I cried when your Hathers died, not for her, but for you. I cried, too, when the twins were born, to see the pain you were in and the length of your labour and my helplessness to help you. When Amadeo was born, I think that was the nearest I ever came to crying hard. It was as though there was to be no end to your contractions, no end to the monitoring of the machine beside you, reflecting your torment on its unreal scan. That machine kept saying that all was well, while you were pleading with the nurses to let you go, to let you off. I heard you bargaining with the ward staff, promising in your delirium never to hide again if only they would stop the pain. I would have cried then, but you needed me more than I needed to cry and I took strength from somewhere, and saw you through.

106

Back in Larenguebec, sharing your attic, I shared your tears and the tears grew into sobs and the sobs became a major fit of weeping.

When I woke up from it, the air had cooled, and I knew that it was much later. You were sleeping, wrapped over me, and shaking, convulsively. I don't know where the twins slept, all those other nights. From what I pieced together later, they slept in a double bed on the floor below. Amadeo, it seemed, was left out in the pram. On that night, though, they had climbed up the last flight of stairs to share your littered room. When I awoke, it was too dark to see, but I heard their steady, childish breathing on the far side of you. I disentangled myself, and noticed that I felt very weak, but at the same time there was a sharpness on my skin. I felt a clearness inside my head. I left you there, sleeping and trembling with our indistinguishable daughters beside you. There were some old rugs in the other attic room, and I covered you with them. Then I took up the last and most precious of all the bundles that you had discarded, and carried him downstairs.

I found his clothes on the first floor in a small room where Amadeo must once have slept, and where, in the words of the twins, he must have 'woken up dead'. There was a battered wooden cot there, with the remains of a pink teddy bear painted on one end and a posy of flowers on the other. I was looking for clean clothes to dress him in, but the sight of the cot upset me. I didn't want to cry – I don't think I could have done any more. I resented even the presence of his barred bed. It was as though the cot had caused the cot death: as though the slats themselves were responsible for the mysterious syndrome that had stolen my son away and tormented my wife. Why should apparently healthy babies die? Why should it have been my child?

I put Amadeo back in the cot, to see if what might have killed him could bring him back to life. I thought I heard my father's heavy voice ringing in my ears, speaking as he used to do from his pulpit, 'And on the third day he rose again from the dead. And did not the angels say when they sought his body, 'Why seek ye the living among the dead? He is not here, but risen' . . . 'Behold my hands and my feet, that it is I myself: handle me, and see; for a spirit hath not flesh and bones, as ye see me have.'

Well, I rummaged in his trunk for a fresh gown, and I found the one with the lace and embroidery. Then I turned back slowly to the

107

cot, hoping that just as I had thought you dead and found you still alive, so Amadeo could speak to me or stir or breathe again, and our life could take its normal course. My head hardly wanted to turn, but it finally did, and he was still there, like a poor soiled effigy of our son. I had to cut his clothes to undress him, and I had to cut his clean clothes to dress him again. Then I lifted him from his cot to find a ritual and a burial for him as it should have begun on his first day of death, however many days ago that was. I wrapped him in a blanket, incongruously, so that he wouldn't catch cold, and then I carried him back out across the footpath to the back garden and up the jagged steps in search of some authority to take my burden from me.

XII

William

When I left that grey stone house in Larenguebec and picked my way through the neglected back garden to report the death of my son, I still believed in an ordered society, and in the authority of the State. I thought all I needed to do to make things normal again was to go back into the village and find the man in charge. I went out to turn my ordinary life back into an ordinary life marred by grief and pockmarked (temporarily) by illness. I was convinced that it could be done. I didn't entirely underestimate the hostility and alienation of the locals. I knew that what I had to say to them would get a fairer hearing without my taking Amadeo with me. I didn't want to frighten or alarm them, I just wanted to break through their closed ranks to the powers that be, or at least, to some kind of bureaucracy.

So I left Amadeo in his pram for one last time, and set off down the winding street in the dark unlit night. The village was deserted. It was only half-past nine by my watch – not by any means an ungodly hour, least of all in France. Yet the cottages were all battened up as though to keep the Devil himself at bay, and there were no lights showing. I couldn't understand why these people went to bed so early, they didn't seem to work particularly. I hadn't seen any signs of fishing from the beach earlier, and the crabs were obviously over-breeding. Whatever the reason for the unnatural hush, I had an emergency to deal with. I needed a doctor for you and Amadeo had to be given a grave.

I knocked firmly on the door of the first cottage on the slope down to the sea. There was no answer. I knocked again, but still nothing happened. Then I tried the next house along, and was again met by silence. I hammered on the door until flecks of dry paint jumped back into my face from the peeling panels. This remitted a noise above my head that developed into a steady cursing, then a shutter was unlatched and the outline of a face joined forces with the voice to abuse me. I stood away from the house so that the man could see me and I spoke out loudly in my schoolboy French. I asked him for the police and a doctor. At the word 'police', he slammed the shutters and disappeared back into the house. Two cottages down, I reversed the order of my requests, putting doctor first and then police. This seemed to make not the slightest difference. The bar was closed, but when I actually managed to bring the sour-faced barmaid down in her dressing-gown to open the door, I was refused the use of the telephone.

I was aware of my own tiredness, and my potential inadequacy for the task ahead of me. I felt somehow terribly hurt by the villagers' rejection. I couldn't look at it in the light of my intrusion into their lives, my foreignness; it was all personal that night. I felt that they didn't like me, blamed me, and had washed their hands of me and my family. Most of all, though, I took their hostility and their anger as a refusal to mourn for my son. I wanted them all to mourn for him. Even though his baby hearse had been trundled up and down their village hill for days carrying his concealed corpse and they had stared and spat at it, I wanted them to grieve for him now. I wanted them to show their last respects for the child that was mine but could have been theirs.

There are times when humanity seems to share a common pool of emotions. There are always some moments of intense communal feeling, when nationality and creed and race pass into second place and the urgency of love or grief has its ascendancy. Even during war, opposing troops have laid down their guns and called a truce to wish each other 'Merry Christmas'. That happened in France, when the soldiers climbed out of the trenches to walk across the frozen mud of no man's land to greet each other. They sang carols together, despite the miles of carnage and barbed wire. If it happened once in France, I felt, why couldn't it happen again? Why couldn't they sense the grieving parent in me and come down to the street, and forget their enmity and draw from their own stock of human feelings enough to care for Amadeo?

I have a stubborn optimism. I wanted this to happen. I wanted their hearts to soften, and for them to prove that they were just men and women, like you and me. I wandered aimlessly up and down that steep village street, long after I had finished knocking. I suppose I was hoping that someone would take pity and do as I had asked, call for an ambulance or the police, or preferably both. The minutes passed and nothing happened, so I stumbled along the lane and over the empty crossroads to the road that led back to civilization. The route looked very different by night and on foot and without the unnatural heat of the previous day.

After about half a mile, I saw a telephone box. I half expected it to be vandalized, but it worked. I dialled the free emergency number and waited to be connected for what seemed like a long time. I wondered what happened when there was a stabbing; did the victim bleed to death waiting for the operator to connect the call? In the end, I didn't get one but three operators. I asked each one in clear, slow French to send an ambulance and the police to an emergency at Larenguebec.

'I'll wait for you at the crossroads,' I said.

At one point I was put through to a man with heavy catarrh who insisted he was in charge of the local police. I arranged to meet him too, after explaining that this was a case of life or death, and then I waited out on the still warm tarmac of the road. I saw a bus stop marked only by a concrete post, and I went to examine it. Despite the thick veil of graffiti over the timetable, I discovered that the next bus wasn't due until Wednesday at six p.m.

I waited restlessly, but nobody came. I felt vulnerable out there on the open road, and I began to fret in case you or the twins might have woken up and be needing me. I hadn't mentioned Amadeo's death on the phone; I don't know why. I didn't want to give the wrong impression before anyone arrived. The more I stood out there, pacing through the dim moonlight, the more I worried about what that wrong impression could do. You were ill, Rosalind, you needed help, professional help, and soon. I sensed that the slightest false move and you could be lost to me, lost to yourself, maybe for ever. I imagined an ambulance manned by the likes of the villagers, treating you roughly, spitting and swearing and somehow accusing you of things. Then I imagined the police, and what their attitude might be. They were not renowned for their tact or understanding. Why had it been so long before the death was reported? How long was it? I didn't know the answers to these questions, and I knew that you must not be asked them in your present state. What did Amadeo die of? They would be sure to ask, and insist on an autopsy, and lacerate your wounds.

The twins lied sometimes, often, but they weren't lying at Larenguebec. I believed them then and, over the years, I still believe them, utterly. I thought that eventually they would discover that Amadeo had died a spontaneous death from the unexplained syndrome that kills babies from birth to two. It is a lethal phenomenon with no warning and no symptoms and no respite for the parents who have put their baby safely to bed the evening before. Yes, eventually, they would sift through the hostile witnesses of Larenguebec and rediscover Candy, wherever she was, and drag her back to the post that she had so callously left when you most needed her, and they would be able to prove beyond all reasonable doubt that you were not responsible for what happened. Perhaps, I projected, they would discover first that you were very ill and needed psychiatric care, or perhaps they would hound you so that you never recovered.

I floundered round the crossroads thinking these things, and I began to fear the arrival of the help I'd called for. I had arranged to meet the ambulance, and the police at the crossroads, to wait for them there, but what if they were really waiting for me? What if they came and finished off the destruction of my family that had begun and seemed to stop, but could so easily continue? They were late, very late, if they were still coming. My mind began to race. It was you and the twins who needed most protection. Amadeo had to be buried, but I could bury him. If they turned up, I thought, what would they do with him, the authorities? They would put his frail body in a plastic bag. I wondered if they would keep his gown on him. I hated, suddenly, the idea of them taking it off. They would lay him on a slab and keep him in the kind of mortuary drawer that I had seen on television. That was where the unresolved deaths' corpses were kept. They would also cut him about. There was a special saw they used to open the skull. I went back down the road and into the phone box, irrationally wanting to get my phone call back. It was as though I thought I could recapture the words I had spoken down the line and take them away with me. I didn't want any strange doctors to further the cause of pathology on my son, or

112

pompous coroners to decide on a case the intricacies of which they could never know. I didn't want any police department to take weeks or even months to discover the truth that I was telling them now. I had a son who had to be buried. Worst of all, I began to fear what would happen if the police didn't believe my story, or the story told by the twins – who were, after all, only eight – or if they couldn't find Candy. I began to fear what they might make of your story. I didn't even know what your story might be. It seemed inconceivable, but the thought began to creep into my brain, that you might actually go to prison through the malice of this place.

I walked back to the house. I'd grown somehow almost as superstitious as the natives of the village. I remember muttering prayers under my breath. They feared the Centrale and the Arabs, and the Evil Eye. I feared the arrival of the police, of an unkind ambulance to manhandle you, of anyone who might witness our loss and our grief and invent guilt from all your wounded innocence. I knew a lot of prayers. I suppose I ought to have, I had grown up with them. Out there in Larenguebec, it was the prayers for the visitation of the sick that came to my mind and that I mumbled as I made my way home. I knew those prayers best, because I always repeated them under my breath when my father dragged me round to visit the sick of his parish. I felt so sorry for those ill people without their strength, who had to bear, as well as their aches and pains, the chiding of my father's pastoral visit. He would arrive, armed with a pound of my mother's home-made pumpkin jam and, in terminal cases, with a jar of pumpkin chutney too. He used to rap on the offending front door and then stride in. He would stand over the sickbed and remind the cowering and remorseful patient that he personally had never had a day's illness in his life. Having thus chided the sick, he would read out two and a half columns of prayers from the Book of Common Prayer in a voice guaranteed in itself to induce a headache. These sick calls would end abruptly with a reminder to the parishioner in question that really ill people died – but only when the Lord was ready to receive them – and that others should get up from their lazy beds and get back to work. He often took their tears as a sign of confession to this shamming. I found that, particulary with the older people, I wanted to make up for my father's hardness. Although he was their vicar, and I was only the vicar's son, I believed that I could atone in some small way if I repeated the prayers, so I did.

When I reached the back garden, I was still whispering,

'I am become as it were a monster unto many: but my sure trust is in thee.

'O let my mouth be filled with thy praise: that I may sing of thy glory and honour all the day long.

'Cast me not away in the time of age: forsake me not when my strength faileth me.

'For mine enemies speak against me, and they that lay wait for my soul take their counsel together, saying: God hath forsaken him, persecute him, and take him; for there is none to deliver him.'

It was all quiet in the house. I ran upstairs to see, but you were still sleeping. I found a full-size garden spade in a cupboard in the kitchen. It seemed a bizarre thing to keep in a kitchen, but I was past wondering. Malkin, our cat, came in through the window and nearly frightened the life out of me. I hadn't fully appreciated that you had taken the cat with you until then. I thought aloud, Mrs King will be furious when she finds out; then I realized that there were more seriuos things to contend with than Mrs King's wrath. I couldn't find a torch, so I took some matches, and then went back outside. I left Amadeo in his pram, as anxious now as the twins had been to keep up appearances. I wheeled him down to the long, far, sandy beach feeling very aware of the moon and the sea, and of there being just my dead son and me and the vestige of a God somewhere, whatever or whoever that God might be.

I was no longer a believer. At some point in my boyhood I had ceased to be, but I accepted the rites, and the order of things, and the ritualized behaviour of life and death. So I wheeled my child down to the sea shore praying, 'Go not far from me, O God: my God, haste thee to help me.' And I kept on saying it, not because I believed in a divine presence there to help me, but because I wanted to believe in the rightness of things, and I wanted Amadeo to be protected long after I went away. I didn't want to abandon him in the sand: I wanted a babysitter more reliable than Candy, more reliable even than Mrs King, to look after him there.

I wheeled the pram along the wet edge of the sand where it was easier to push it. I must have walked for about a mile before I came to a small cove of rocks set back from the sea, and I decided to bury him there. Even as I pushed my way along the beach, I was aware of doing something illegal, but when I asked myself whether it was wrong, the answer was always the same. I was looking after you, looking after Amadeo and the twins, I was doing the best I could. That was all any of us did there, the best we could. I appreciate that an outsider might fail to understand my motives, but I know, because I heard you scream and I saw you there and I know how much you loved Amadeo, and I know that you are not to blame for what happened. After I buried him, the only person in our family who had actually committed a crime was me. I had unlawfully buried a human child. After that, not you, but I, would take any blame that might be coming. There is so much prejudice against mental illness; so much prejudice against the unexplained in general. No court of law would have found it easy to accept your mental state and that cot death without some snide and vicious questions about the details of it all. I was just so frightened, Rosalind, that something bad would happen to you.

I dug a very deep grave, it was much bigger than it needed to be, but that was the only way I could make it really deep. I wondered as I dug what the police would have to say about the twins and their grave-digging. I thought about a lot of things as I dug that pit. When the moment came to lay Amadeo in it, I felt an urge to keep him with us for a few more days. I remembered my father's stern voice urging mourning parents to draw back from the edge of a grave so that the first clods of Norfolk clay could be thrown down on to a coffin and the sextons could fill up the hole. I made my father's voice draw me back now from holding on to my grey-eyed son, I didn't want to tip sand into his eyes. He never liked sand in his eyes, so I climbed in after him and covered his face with my handkerchief. I thought as I did so that the handkerchief could be traced back to me. It was initialled and English, and, if it were ever found, it would incriminate me. I realized that I didn't care, because I never wanted to disown Amadeo. I would be glad to suffer whatever price a father has to suffer for his son. All that kept me from burying him in a proper piece of consecrated ground was time. I needed the time to protect the living, and the time had to be forfeited from the dead. I would never deny him. I thought as I buried him that, if his body were to be found and a hunt begun, I would go out to France and claim his corpse and name his remains and not let any further disrespect come to him.

As I pushed the empty pram back over the beach to the house, I didn't feel like a criminal. I thought about it briefly, but I could hardly feel anything; just a numbness at the back of my head, and an awareness of the cold breeze blowing in from the sea. There was a bad smell still, all the way back. I couldn't really deal with it. My mind had had enough for one night. Every time the pram jogged, I smelt it again.

One of my colleagues in the graphics firm that I worked for had a schizoid sister. They shared a flat somewhere in Holland Park. She worked for some photographer, and I believe she was very good at her job. At parties and things, she used to call herself the 'model assistant'. I hadn't thought about her all year, but somehow she came to mind as I wheeled back the pram, and I remembered that she had had a schizophrenic episode about twelve months before. She had telephoned our office, and told her brother that the photographer had forced his cameras and lenses into her shin bones. She had claimed that she was hiding in a phone box, because he was looking for her to make her swallow his tripod. She was sent for treatment to a clinic in Switzerland. We all took an interest at the firm, in the course of her illness, from the tea boy to the directors. I suppose there wasn't much to talk about sometimes as we worked; and also I think we had all found the message amusing when we first heard it, and by talking about her with sympathy later, we expiated our guilt. I rummaged in my tired brain for the name of the clinic that had cured her, and that I hoped could cure you, Rosalind. I am usually good with names; I was amazed when I first met you, and we started spending time together, how you could arrive somewhere, check into a hotel, go for a walk, and completely forget where you were staying. You told me that you had sometimes spent whole days hunting through strange towns for your particular pension.

I eventually remembered the name of that clinic, and by some strange feat I remembered the phone number of Monsieur Laurent, who had driven me out to Larenguebec the previous morning. I felt tempted to get hold of him right away and arrange for our retreat from that wretched place. However, it was four o'clock in the morning, and I didn't have any money on me for the call. In a film, I thought, the hero would always have a dime in his pocket for a call. Then I remembered that this wasn't a film, or even a dream, and I started running, and I kept running up the hill until I got back to you.

I was afraid that something else had happened. I was living suddenly in your 'world of the cleaver'. I felt its blade hovering over us. I feared the late arrival of police and ambulance, but they never came – I still don't know why. When I went upstairs, I found you asleep as I'd left you, with the twins curled up on your left-hand side. The sun was already rising when I lay down beside you. I was lulled to sleep almost immediately by your presence, which became in my dreams like the lulling of the sea. I heard again the waves slapping on the shore. I felt them dragging out the last of Amadeo, taking his spirit down into their depths. The sea moved by its own tides regardless of any human rules. It was in direct contact with the moon and the stars. It could seem like a liquid shadow of the moon. You can lure and lull, too. You are like two sisters, but the sea doesn't pause to take notice of me.

So I was lulled into a deep sleep, from which I woke some five hours later to guide you all away from that catastrophic holiday. The same taxi took us back to Cherbourg. The driver was so relieved not to have to haul the pram on to his already scratched roof that he didn't even ask about the baby. The twins were talkative by spurts on the journey, and you encouraged them, pointing out this and that in the countryside. At the end of the ride, the driver congratulated you on the improvement in your health.

'I was quite worried about you,' he confessed, 'but you look a lot more relaxed now.' Then he thought a moment, and added, 'I never thought of Larenguebec as a resort before; but I suppose it takes all sorts.'

From Cherbourg we took the train to Dijon and then across the Alps to Switzerland. I took you to the clinic where the schizophrenic girl had been cured. You seemed well then, and the twins seemed well. It was a relief to see how suddenly you appeared to have recovered from the delusions and the bells. I didn't dare mention the baby until you did. I tried to relax too, but I was waiting for the cleaver to fall. I had a lump in my throat whenever I thought about Amadeo, sand, crabs, cuttle-fish or even the sea. I missed him, and I was afraid for you. I felt that you couldn't see the danger, the slim potential danger of your son being exhumed in Normandy. So in my mind I was always running. I was running away from the police and from enquiring stares and from too many questions and details. Most of all, though, I was running away from my grief.

XIII

Rosalind

It was strange going back to London. Willie and I flew alone, and it seemed like ages since I had travelled without the twins. We went to visit them before we left. When I saw them in the school uniforms, I felt a glow of pride. It was as though they had both been made honorary doctors for me. I'm sure, one day, they'll do something very clever with their lives – everyone says that they're so gifted. I sometimes got the feeling during the summer that they were regressing to their natural age. I was too hazy at the time to remember at what point they changed, but there was a helplessness about them. I noticed immediately we went in that they had won the heart of their headmistress; so much so, that she insisted on coming round the school and grounds with us, and never left us a moment's privacy.

I read a school story once when I was a child about a boarding school in Switzerland. I remember that it had a blue cover, and everyone in it drank mugs of cocoa, and one of the girls was a spoil-sport, and they all knew how to ski. At one point, the heroine, a courageous twelve-year-old, was spanked by a man with a beard. That book held a strange fascination for me. As I walked around the twins' new school, I was disappointed not to find dozens of used mugs with cocoa skins and grease sticking to them, and I was immensely relieved that there was no one with a beard on the premises.

The floors were tremendously highly polished. They had the sort of shine that Mrs King used to dream about and claimed that she knew from her youth. I had polished my shoes that day, and as we filed along the corridors, the headmistress said, 'We like the girls to acquire polish.' Outside, behind the main building, a groundsman was cleaning the cars with a kind of spray-on wax. I was glad that the girls were going to a coherent place.

The headmistress, a Miss Juniper, walked just in front of me, to one side. Each time she thought of something else to say, she would wheel about, almost tripping up the entire procession. I'd never actually met the headmistress of a girls' boarding school before, but, even at the time, I thought that this one was too good to be true. If someone had put her in a film, she would have been criticized for being unrealistic, and yet she was a sort of living caricature from some 1940s comic. Miss Juniper was tall, and I never really like women to be taller than me. But she won so clearly with her six foot two to my five foot eleven that I let it go. She was also very thin, in a kind of jaunty athletic way that some older women are. I think she must have been in her late fifties. A few strands of her hair were beginning to turn grey, but, on the whole, she had indiscriminately brown hair with that natural ashen hue that defies all attempts to enhance it. It was completely straight, and again this was hard to believe in. I remembered that in my distant childhood, girls had ironed their hair to get the correct 'Mod' effect. I couldn't quite picture Miss Juniper here with her head sideways on an ironing board, flattening her hair every morning before assembly, but it didn't look natural at all.

William and the twins seemed to have grown suddenly close. They had always had a slightly difficult relationship at home because the twins insisted on winding him up. Anyone with a nature less sweet than his would have gone off them years ago, but Willie just persevered, and I was pleased to see that they had finally let him be close to them. I could hear them behind me, chattering to him, and even talking separately, which was a great and rare honour. Merging with their conversation behind me were Miss Juniper's breathlessly enthusiastic remarks, which in their turn seemed to muddle into one long speech.

'We insist on two vegetables with each meal, and one of them must be green. Of course, leek and lentil make up meat. Baths are on Mondays, Wednesdays and Saturdays, and all the girls have to wear gloves to church. There must be three at a time, one to bandage a knee and one to dash for help. French, of course, is a must . . .'

Her voice seemed to drone into all the doorways and catch on all the stairs. In the main hall, over the front door, there was a portrait of a young girl leaning on a balustrade and wearing white lace gloves. I was glad that she was wearing gloves, I was too, and as a result I felt reassured that the twins would be looked after properly.

I am sure that I must have seen a wombat before, but maybe only a picture of one, because I thought they were about ten times bigger than they turned out to be. The twins were thrilled, showing me around the wired-in plot of ground that formed their antipodean garden, and they obviously knew far more about wombats than I did. I felt vague misgivings to see the dwarfed size of these creatures. I suggested to Miss Juniper that these particular wombats might be much happier if they were to be released. I just didn't like to see them lolloping around their little patch of defecated mud. From somewhere behind me the school bell rang, and, with it, the old bells started ringing in my head. I felt, simultaneously, tears welling in my eyes, and the twins freezing with embarassment to the patch of ground where they were standing, and William rushing round to my rescue.

I used to think that I was William's rescuer. He lived in such a hard, matter-of-fact world before I met him, and I saved him from that. My life gets to be like a James Bond film, though, when it comes to the number of times that William has rescued me. There are the big times and the little times, but it's when details explode that I'm hurt the most. So I was as grateful to be dragged away by him from the twins' school and the pet wombats as I was for being steered away from Larenguebec. I was thankful, too, when he took me away from the clinic, and back home to the autumnal crush of London and Tanza Road.

It would have disturbed me to have seen my report from the clinic. When I was a child, I used to dream of getting a report at the end of each school term. I suppose it was a bit like having name tapes and a tuck box – it was a status symbol in my eyes. It meant that you were an accepted member of society – any society – instead of a lone girl kept locked up with two eccentric women in a rambling cobwebbed house. I could never bring myself to ask Hathers to write a report. It wouldn't have been inappropriate really, but I wasn't sure if she was capable of it. It's ironic that as a child I worried about Hathers being able to write a report, while, leaving Switzerland, I worried about my being able to read one. I knew that it would list my eccentricities and interpret them as signs of madness.

Hathers didn't have many jokes, but when she did get hold of one she would flog it almost to death. She discovered the following one when I was about seven, and it used to rock her with paroxysms of laughter. She would lean forward and purse her lips slightly and smile to herself, already anticipating what was to come. Then she'd say, 'Ros?'

'Yes.'

'What's the first sign of madness?'

Even though I knew the answer, and she knew that I did, I would wait for a few seconds before telling her, 'Hairs on the palms of your hands.'

Then I'd stroke my hands together a little while I waited for her to say, 'And what's the second sign?'

When I was seven, I used to think that it would ruin her fun if I told her this second answer, so I would just shrug. By the time I was about thirteen, I knew that it made no different to her enjoyment whether I shared it or not, and so I'd say, 'Looking for them.'

At which she would drop whatever she was holding, stop whatever she was doing and rock her thick frame backwards and forwards shouting, 'You just did, you just did!'

As I sat on the aeroplane going back from Geneva to Gatwick, I thanked God that I had had the presence of mind to conceal this incident from the prying eyes of the psychiatrists. I imagined that they already had ample idiocies of mine to deal with and account for without adding unnecessarily to their score. Every time that I was struck by some coincidence of speech or gesture or the significance of a recurring object, I felt myself sinking deeper and deeper into a clinical classification, and further and further away from my real self. I always feel that it doesn't bear thinking about too closely at times what that 'real self' might be, and who, but who wants to be a mere set of figures on a computer?

Mummy and Uncle Jeremy were always commenting on similar

things that came about by chance. Uncle Jeremy was very paranoid about them, while Mummy just noticed. I tried telling one of the nurses this, but her eyes seemed to glaze over at the thought of any genetic explanation for my supposed madness. When I stop and think about it – which seems to be rather often at the moment – I can't see why everybody is so ashamed of insanity. Whether it's temporary, permanent, or whatever, why is it such a big deal? And who is everybody? Why do I mind talking to a shrink? The word isn't synonymous with a child molester or a cannibal, so what is so taboo about it all?

Perhaps shrink is the wrong term here. Because it is really the 'men in white coats' who still bear the stigma. Everybody has an analyst nowadays. Even children are getting to be nobody if they don't have problems. It's like establishing credit in a bank. If you borrow money and you pay it back, you're a nice client. So, you have problems, you get them straightened out, and that makes you a co-operative member of the world corporation. It's just when *they* call *you*. Just the reverse of showbiz, because when it comes to the state of your head, it's only all right if you call them. The day the male nurses come for you, you're a loser, a marginal person, a walker of the barbed-wire zone.

As I sat on the aeroplane, it was the implications of my illness that I resented. When the air hostess asked if I wanted a sick bag, I felt deeply insulted and somehow betrayed. It seemed that the airline had been running their radio controls over my private file in that Swiss clinic and now they knew that I was unstable. The air hostess knew that I had tripped up once and hurt myself, and that now I might fall again any time. I looked into her unsmiling blue eyes and felt that she could sense a potential relapse in the stuffy air of the Club cabin.

Once, when the twins were newly born and I was struggling with the unfamiliar demands of new motherhood, my agent called from New York. He didn't often call, he usually wrote. He had a way of sending the perfect zany note. I had been working hard; a lot harder really than I felt capable of. I had been pushing myself for months and months, just forcing myself to take more parts and be in more places and give more interviews than I really had the will or the energy to do. Getting pregnant was strange for me. I wanted to have a child, and, I suppose, most of all I wanted to be a good mother to make up for all the loneliness and confusion of my own childhood, and make my own child happy.

I took it upon myself to prove that creativity and childbirth could be accomplished simultaneously; and I honestly feel that they can. I was on the defensive, though, with a pack of Jeremiahs prophesying doom. So I couldn't let well alone. I couldn't act and pass through the months of my gestation without pushing my luck. Instead, I took tens of thousands of vitamins, and accepted virtually every female role for the under forties going, and I tired myself to a shred. It was very much a secret shred. Nobody knew – how could they? – I was carrying twins. I hear people saying, 'Oh, I was so big when I was pregnant with Johnny, or Billy, or Jane.' I wasn't big, I was enormous. It really made me laugh at the time to think that I had been concerned about conealing my waistline. By the time I was seven months gone, I was more concerned with preserving some kind of human identity. The twins each weighed seven and a half pounds, and I think that if they hadn't been born a month premature, I would have burst.

Even after I became so gross I couldn't appear full frontal, profile or even from behind on the screen, I still sold my face. There's a whole fleet of photographs of me from the neck down; and somewhere a lot of cut prints of my massive girth. It seems very appropriate that the chalk mark that a model stands on to have her photograph taken is called 'the idiot line'. I stood on that idiot line for seven years. I couldn't lay my hand on my heart and swear that I wasn't an idiot before I got on it, but I certainly was by the time I stepped off.

I used to whinge about Milton, my agent, but I was actually very fond of him. An actress can get into a lot of trouble without one, and I knew it. So I was grateful to him. Mostly, though, he seemed like a gentleman and a nice person. I really liked him. Colleagues of mine would get tremendously annoyed when I said this. They'd say, 'How can a theatrical agent be a gentleman? It's a contradiction in terms.' I maintained that one had slipped through the net and was personified in London, New York, Los Angeles and Rome, in the guise of Milton himself.

Something happened when the girls were born. It was like a

last-minute reluctance to let them go. I had conceived and carried them, but, when the contractions actually came, I wanted to hold them back, to protect them from so many things. I heard the doctor and the nurses telling me to push, and I felt the pain somewhere: I couldn't even tell where it was; it just hurt and I held back. I thought I was going to die of pain, but a voice inside me told me to hold back. It was like a gruesome game, and we played it for hours. There was a machine monitoring my progress and I remember that it marked my contractions like horses galloping across a screen. There was a strange sound coming from it, and each contraction made it pound so that it sounded like a crush of passengers stampeding off the Staten Island ferry. Somehow it got inside my veins, and I felt the people rushing to get out of me. I feared that there would be nothing left if I let so many people go, so I held them back. I had to think of the early martyrs, and the suffering that they went through for their faith, to give me strength.

I spent eleven hours in fast labour with two-minute intervals between the contractions and then something inside me snapped. I don't remember what happened next until I came round and with a drip in my arm, a plastic cot on either side of my bed, and William beside me. Sometimes I don't want to remember things. When I close my eyes, I can see a man with eyes like my Uncle Bertie – kind, gentle eyes that could be stern – and a green cap and mask standing over me. I was trying to save my babies. I felt myself dying and yet I still wanted to protect them. There were bad things in the hospital that had upset me. I saw the man's eyes twice, he was the surgeon. I saw his nice eyes and then I saw him frown, he was coming towards me. He had me tied to the table with plaster, he could do anything to me. I couldn't see over my huge stomach. I looked up to the ceiling. I was too tired to struggle any more, so I looked up to pray. Then I saw the circular mirror high over me, and I saw in it that the man with the mask was going to stab me. They had given me drugs and I was unclear in my brain, I thought. I reasoned quickly with myself. Why should this stranger want to stab me? He did, though, and he was aiming at my babies. I didn't care any more about the pain. It was in my ideas now, because I didn't want to believe that anyone would do such a thing. But I had seen it happen and the knife was over me, coming down. All this happened in one split second, and then the anaesthetic came.

Later I learnt that Caesarian sections are often performed in that way, to protect the baby from taking in anaesthetic. At the time, though, there was just me, and the knife, and my paranoia. Even when the twins were well and happy, I felt guilty. If they got gripe, or cried, or any little thing went wrong, I used to get in a panic. William had bought a lot of books on childcare. Some of them were very helpful, but none of them seemed to deal with my panic and my guilt and the tremendous inadequacy I felt when they cried. That is not to say that these books didn't mention similar symptoms, they did; but they made them seem insignificant and transitory, whereas mine were locked into my bloodstream.

I virtually didn't see anyone for months after the twins were born, and when I did, I pretended that everything was fine. My face used to ache from forcing a smile on those occasions, because, really, I just wanted to cry.

I used to spend most of my time weeping in those days. Life became like a perennial matinée. I found it strange that I hardly ever cried in real life, while I could soak my hankie with tears on the flimsiest pretext in a film. Giving birth was like taking the pin out of a water grenade. I wasn't safe afterwards. Everything was a potential cause of tears. I had an obsession about inherited neglect. I read a booklet about child abuse, and discovered that trained observers could tell which post-natal mothers were in danger of battering their children just by looking at them. One sentence in particular, about 'the hereditary factor', seemed to engrave itself on my mind. I became convinced that I had inherited from my mother her unerring neglect. Whenever these words reminded me that I was an emotional failure, I would lock myself in the third-floor lavatory and weep. This same booklet on child abuse, which was American in origin, had also described certain parents as being 'way off beam'.

I had always been struck by this phrase. It seemed like such an accurate way of verbalizing an emotional state. I kept this thin but impressive booklet hidden behind the spare lavatory paper in that third-floor loo. Sometimes, when I had cried and then stopped, I would feel that I hadn't wept enough, and then I would thumb through the relevant paragraphs on neglect until my guilt and fears were almost unbearable. I kept the book hidden because I knew that it didn't really apply to me, and I was ashamed of my respnose to it. Also, I was embarrassed to admit to what extent the births had disturbed me and how seriously tired I was. Crying was my secret way of struggling through and the book was my trigger; not even I really believed I was as bad as it implied. Or rather, it was about a different set of people altogether.

When Milton telephoned from New York, I was having a bad day. William was home late, and the nanny had gone out to buy some gripe water and seemed to have disappeared into the fifth dimension. I had never been alone with the twins before, and they were crying. I tried to comfort them, and failed. After a few minutes, I too was crying, but their wails outnumbered mine. I could only carry one because of my recent Caesarian scar which refused stubbornly to heal. When I held one baby, the other still cried, and I felt an overriding sense of unfairness. Eventually, after juggling with their shawls and gowns for some minutes, I decided to leave them both in their brass crib while I forced myself to relax. It was at that moment that Milton telephoned, and his secretary announced the name of his theatrical agency and then left an empty line awaiting his voice.

In the past he had always been on my side. I admit that I recruited his services behind his back, but, in my mind, he was with me against the rest of the world. Meanwhile, though, I had stopped acting, and the 'word' on the street was that I was refusing to go back. I freely confess that the word originated with me. I felt that I'd been very loyal to Milton and that now he should bear with me. Had he been there, he would have seen that I was not in a fit state to be told off or advised professionally about anything. Not least, he would have seen that my eyes were absurdly swollen from crying and that I was a nervous wreck. However, the telephone is entirely impersonal and, because he was feeling strong and determined, he assumed that I was too.

Milton was a gentleman. Was, is, he hasn't changed. He didn't say anything to me that was rude or brusque or, within the parameters of normal life, even unpleasant. And yet, unwittingly, he said the one thing I couldn't bear to hear. He said, 'Rosalind, this is not the time to do this. I have a tremendous respect for you, and I wouldn't say it if I didn't know, but you are way off beam.'

I responded with a horrified silence. How could Milton, who was in New York and couldn't even see me, know that I was so off beam? If he knew, everyone must know. Somehow I had transmitted this down the line. Now everything else that the book said would come true. I couldn't hear what else he said, I couldn't talk clearly either. I wanted him to say things were all right. He had put his finger on my weak place, and suddenly he was the only person who could make me sane again. He kept on, thinking that we were having a business call. As far as I was concerned, we were discussing my ability to survive as a person. We were assessing my chances of ever pulling through. Even as I spoke, I felt an irrational fear of his voice. I tried to pull myself together, but it kept coming down the line.

'You're way off beam, you are way off beam.'

Why was he repeating it? It had to be that he knew.

When the agency nanny returned with the gripe water for the twins, I was prostrate with grief on my bed. I was incapable of telling her what it was about. I couldn't even speak I was so racked by sobs. She had never seen me cry like that before. She called William at his office, and he returned to find me still shaking from my spasms, but sedated now by our family doctor. His first reaction was to assume that the nanny had done something to upset me. I felt too cried out to talk, but, when I saw that he was actually going to sack her, I told him that it wasn't her, it was Milton from New York.

'What did he say?' William demanded.

'Nothing, it was private . . . nothing.'

I saw him thinking, 'How can nothing do this to you?' I was too tired to explain. I don't know if I could have made him understand then; it was a long story, maybe as long as my whole life, who knows.

That phone call and its aftermath became my all time low. Afterwards, everything began to get better. I wanted to tell Milton that he had left his mark on me, but I couldn't even bring myself to apologize – my pride kept asking me, what for? – let alone intensify our relationship, so we drifted apart.

When someone makes you feel like that, there is as close a bond as after making love. It is a kind of love, I suppose. Not many people have made their mark on me. When I count them up, like old lovers, there is Hathers, and Mummy, Uncle Bertie, then Willie, the children, and Angelo, and incongruously there is Milton.

XIV
Rosalind

Sometimes I feel as though I was born in Sestri Levante because I lived my life through a veil before I came here. There were always veils of protection, and veils of pretence, and occasionally they overlapped. I can still remember, when we honeymooned here, the tremendous thrill I got from stepping from one world into another and still being able to step back again. I could leave the wide tourist beach with its ordered palms and its restaurants on the far side of the esplanade, and discover a dream world in the Bay of Silence. There was a square with a broad white church for Santa Maria di Nazareth. It had two squat bell towers with twin sets of stained bronze bells.

The smart clothes and the wealth, backed by the frequent appeals of those bells to Catholicism, were like my past. They were the tangible world of success, and they were all that was superficial in me: my mask. The narrow, flagged passageway that joined that part of Sestri to the other bay was like an allowed access to the hidden me. I used to step from the bustle of one side of the town to the eerie calm of the other and feel as though I was going to die of confusion. Even the sands were different colours. The tourist beach had coarse, black sand, while the Bay of Silence had fine, tawny sand that caught in the sheltered breeze and filled my pockets and my shoes.

I don't know what made *me* famous rather than the girl next door (had there been one). Perhaps it was Milton working hard on my behalf; perhaps I was lucky and the time was right. It always surprised me to read in the press about my 'calm'. Hardly an

128

interview began without dwelling on my 'inner calm'. I used to get very upset about it. I realize now that what was described then as inner calm made others feel calm inside. Meanwhile my mask concealed a ferment of disturbed emotions. What made Sestri Levante so important to me was that I found my own centre there, through Angelo, my angel of redemption.

It still took me years after Angelo disappeared to come to terms with certain things, but he gave me back the will to want to deal with them. Before I met him, I was almost incapable of living moments as they came. The past and the future would always irrevocably drown out the present for me. If they were to be weighed in a scale, then the past was the heaviest. I carried a burden of guilt and responsibility with me. Angleo showed me, as by a vision, how to limit the range of my responsibility to its natural boundary, and to do my best in all things, and having tried my best to be satisfied.

On good days, I lived in my own aura of no regrets. On bad days, for many years to come, I still sank under those shifting sands of blame and guilt. Why was my Uncle Bertie ostracized and banished to Australia if not for me? Why had Hathers died so alone? Why did my mother get cancer if not through her mortification? I worked very hard to involve myself in this mortification of hers, but it was hard to do. She never felt close to me, she wasn't that type of woman. She lived in the world of her face and her friends and I was alien to it. I accept that now. I've done it too. When I was younger I tried to ingratiate myself with her, not realizing that she didn't dislike me as I imagined, she just wasn't interested. I could have disembowelled myself over the banisters and had less effect than a last-minute calcellation of a dinner party. I wasn't in her life, I merely came out of it, and that was that. There were always other guilts, though, to creep in and take her place.

I need Italy with its long siestas and its ritualized families. I need its love of children and its naturalness. I see now that I need Sestri too, not just for the memory of Angelo, but for its geographic mechanism that allows me to relax. I can step across the peninsula and move from the complex to the simple and vice versa at will. I need the sound of the sea on either side of me, and William and all these chocolate éclairs and nice wines and the fruit and big lunches. I think about it, and it's almost embarrassing, the life we lead here.

Which just goes to show, as William always says, that it's a dog's life.

There are a lot of dogs in Sestri Levante. In particular, I have noticed a number of cocker spaniels. I find it strange that I haven't seen more dogs just wandering around or sitting under the oleanders. What is odd is that there are what can only be described as extravagant piles of ordure on the streets and pavements; mostly on the pavements. So that somewhere, a corresponding number of dogs must be lying low.

Bad smells make me glaze over. I used to glaze over all the time. I could tell when I was doing it with Willie, because he'd say, 'Ahoy there' or start waving. Or he'd get his Jimmy voice to call me back from wherever I had drifted off to. God knows how often I used to do it with other people. I expect Hathers never noticed it, not least because she drifted off so often herself. As for Mummy, she rarely saw me, and she was what Father Ingot used to call the most volatile member of the parish. I hardly ever glaze over now, but there are some things that I am not prepared to think about. Mrs King used to say that her memory played tricks on her. Mine doesn't exactly play tricks, it just refuses to recall certain people, or places, or events. I think it is better like that. I feel happy with things as they are.

In Luasanne, I'd thought that Willie was laying it on a bit thick with all his concern for my 'fragile state of mind'. He must have told the doctors that I had a phobia about hospitals, because they all insisted on whispering to me so that I wouldn't think they were shouting. Some of them just spoke very quietly, which made our conversations a bit trying if they turned their heads away for so much as a second. Others, though, whispered in broken English, with the natural strains of their French and German coming through. It made me feel as though I was in transit in some modern zoo. When I got back to the house in Tanza Road, I felt wary of all our friends. Even the house worried me. I missed the twins so much that I felt a hollowness inside me. Sometimes I could remember the dark, but I didn't want to, and William helped me. I admired him again as I had done when I first met his mother in Norfolk. He was a man who had a lot to put up with. I was scarred, and the scars ached. I wanted them to heal; then I wanted to help Willie to get over his fears.

Every time Mrs King asked after the twins, no sooner had I opened my mouth to tell her about them in their new Swiss school than Willie leapt in and began to speak in chorus with me.

There were a lot of sad things in our house. I looked along the row of Beatrix Potter books, the frieze of the Shaker alphabet all painted with pastel animals and flowers, and the toys, and I felt sad. And I felt sad when I saw the painted chairs with swans on their backs. I began to banish all these things from their rooms. Anything that suggested babyhood was locked away in the junk room. There was a phantom baby locked in my brain but I had to black out the details. When I searched my mind, I found no answers. Details can kill. My Uncle Bertie used to say that there were more casualties during the first year of the last war in England due to the black-out than due to enemy action. Whenever I tried to find a way through the labyrinth of my memory and was met by darkness, I remembered the wartime story. I could imagine cars driving slowly through the black night with their headlights out, mowing down pedestrians and crashing into other cars.

I liked the darkness, but not to search through it. Saint Anthony is the patron saint of lost things. Hathers used to invoke him regularly for her thimble, her spectacles and missing pieces of jigsaw puzzles. Hathers felt the cold, so she used to wear cardigans all the year round. Whenever we were doing a puzzle, she had a way of reaching across the table to examine a piece and knocking off dozens of other bits with the cuff of her knitted sleeve. I mused that perhaps Saint Anthony would know what I had done with my lost memories and why. But he was a saint plagued by other requests, and I felt that it would be better just to lay the toys to rest.

William told our friends and Mrs King that there had been a car crash in France and that I was in a state of shock, and mustn't be spoken to about it. So no one mentioned the twins to me and whenever the subject of babies arose, it was suddenly hushed in an embarrassed silence. After a while I didn't want to see our friends any more. It was as though their failure to understand could hurt me. William too had become constrained in their company. Even Mrs King had changed. She had taken to wandering around the house in a mournful way with her redundant feather duster. Occasionally her tongue would get the better of her and she'd blame the

'Frenchies' for the emptiness of our house. One day, while I was making myself a cup of coffee, she said, 'It's a cryin' shame. I have to say it. That's what it is. The Germans was too good for them.'

At this point the coffee that I was making boiled over and splashed the previously immaculate stove.

'Well,' she said, mopping up the stains, 'the only good thing is we got rid of Candy.'

Mrs King had never disguised her scorn and dislike of our nanny, but she wiped the stove with such a vitriolic grinding of her wrist and teeth that I was quite startled.

'I hate them Frenchies,' she said. 'Mr Walsh told me not to say nothing, but it rankles.'

As the months wore on, and Willie became more and more nervous with Mrs King, and Mrs King became more and more frustrated in her work with us, I saw little of her. On the occasions when we did see each other she didn't mention the crash again. She merely told me how much she missed Fred, Willie's tortoise. She pronounced the word 'tortoys'.

She told me, 'You don't find tortoises like that Fred every day. You should have seen him with a lettuce leaf. He was a hooligan with a bit of lettuce was that Fred.'

XV

William

Before we came to Italy, I used to lie awake at night wondering what would happen if Candy ever met Mrs King again. This was only a remote possibility, given their differing ages and tastes; not least because Mrs King was quite capable of refusing to speak to her on the street, and this scorn was not entirely unreturned. Yet a demon in my mind would wake me up at night and say, 'Yes, but what if they met on a train? What if Candy came back to Tanza Road for her things and my invention of a car crash was exposed?' For it was undeniable that after she disappeared with her Guernseyman from Laranguebec, Candy never returned to collect her accumulated belongings from her many years of idle nannying with us.

At one point, immediately after we left France, I wanted her to come back. She was our one witness. In the event of a charge or trial, she was the only person who could corroborate the twins' story, and swear that Amadeo had died a simple cot death. I don't know why I made up the story of a crash. It was a stupid thing to do. I could have said pneumonia or meningitis or anything else that can happen in bed. But I wanted to explain your fragility too. So I came up with the tale of a road accident. Our respective families were dead and our friends were shocked and sympathetic, so nobody questioned it. Nobody would, really – except for Candy. It didn't dawn on me for some time, though, that my story to Mrs King could jeopardize everything if Candy did come back. Meanwhile, I put advertisements for her in dozens of newspapers. These were non-committal appeals to her better nature. It was a surprise for me to see that nobody found the absence of our children in the least suspicious. I expect if just one child had been missing, it might have seemed sinister, but with three children and their nanny all gone, and you newly out of a clinic and still convalescing, no one asked after them.

However, as one month followed the next, then whole seasons passed, I realized that I no longer wanted Candy to come back, ever. Where before I had longed to make things technically straight again, I came to yearn only to be allowed to forget. And most of all for you to live unmolested by memories that might still unhinge your mind. There was nobody to re-open our wound, nor to disturb the sand; nobody, that is, except Candy.

I grew to fear her return more than anything else. I was in her power, and I hated it. I spent months and months worrying about it. I would lie awake at night imagining all the different forms that a discovery could take. The more I worried about it, the more uneasy I felt; and I began to fear Mrs King, because she knew my lie, and could, potentially, destroy the balance of our lives. Sometimes, it seemed that her questions were more knowing than she let on. Hardly a day would go by without her asking about Fred. I thought, given that I had told her I didn't know what had happened to my tortoise, why didn't she accept my word? The fact that I was lying to her didn't make me feel any better about her refusal to believe me. Precisely because I was lying, it was more important that she did.

Tortoises hibernate, they get run over, they even get lost, so why did Mrs King insist on dwelling on the loss of Fred? On my more paranoid days, I thought she did it solely to unnerve me. I fantasized meetings between her and Candy, with the latter telling her how the tortoise got forgotten in the pram. On other days, resentment took over from my fear. It was, after all, my tortoise and not hers, and I missed him more than she did; but I had a son to mourn, and I was unable to get as excited over Fred. One day, when I just couldn't stand the subject any longer, I told her that I found it distasteful and that I didn't want to hear another word about it. After that, every time she introduced the topic, she did so with an aggrieved sigh and an, 'I know it doesn't matter to some . . . but things aren't the same here without Fred. When I think of the way he could . . .'

All through my life, whenever things got really bad for me, I would see the world in terms of symbols. After our return from Switzerland, I drifted deeper and deeper into this device. Sometimes I interpreted what I did and saw in terms of symbols within the context of my real life; and sometimes I translated them into imaginary scenarios which I changed and adjusted according to my mood. At school, I had lived through my first, tormented year almost entirely in the invisible guise of Tin Tin, the intrepid detective. In Tanza Road, I managed to avoid the French sleuth, and his incompetent friends, the Thompson Twins, but the peripheral symbolism of that make-believe life remained. As a child, where Tin Tin had his faithful dog, Snowy, to assist him in his hours of need, I had my loyal tortoise, Fred.

By the time Mrs King came to miss him, Fred had been with me, I suppose, for over twenty years. I hadn't been allowed any pets at home. Mother didn't approve of them. I used to want a dog more than anything else in the world, when I was a boy. It seemed most pressing when I was living at the rectory, then, after I went to boarding school, I dreamt of coming home to a Lassie-like fondness instead of the disapproving murmurs of my parents. I was so obsessed by this project that I even broached it, twice, with my father. On each occasion, he said, simply, 'As a dog returneth to his vomit, So a fool returneth to his folly.'

My next plan was for a cat. Our house used to be overrun by mice, and a cat, I thought, could slip under Mother's portcullis by despatching a few. Mother was not impressed. She said that mousetraps were cleaner, more efficient, ate nothing and didn't get fleas. Plan forty-three was the capture and taming of a mouse. This lasted for two weeks before mother became suspicious and ransacked my room. I then attempted to keep a pet bird. My record here was with a starling that lived under my smothering attentions for a miraculous six days; and that was the end of my attempts to keep a pet in the house. I was at the height of despair over this failure, when our doddering but kindly gardener came to my rescue.

For longer than I could remember, he had gardened for us, and he had always seemed tremendously old. I don't know what his age really was, but he outlived both of my parents and still lives in Norfolk, I believe, in his dank cottage with his cough and his decrepit blind dog, and his mouldering bunches of herbs. Nobody could rightfully accuse my father of favouritism, not even I, his son, or his neighbours, or his worst enemy. The Reverend Walsh was fair in all things, including his unfairness. Thus he treated me with the same harshness that he used to my mother, and all his parishioners and also, his gardener, Mr Gotobed. Had this Mr Gotobed seemed even a little younger, I would have found his surname amusing, but, as it was, he looked as though if he ever went to bed, he might never rise again. Despite his name, though, and his apparent senility, he came and reported for work twice a week at the rectory.

No matter how early he came, Father would always be up and out earlier. On the rare occasions when he arrived a few minutes late for work, on exceptionally wet or snowy days, Father would lecture him like a truant schoolboy. None of these threats and slights ever seemed to make the slightest impression on our aged employee. This was not least because of his deafness and the broad dialect of his own Norfolk speech, so remote from Father's clipped southernisms. The one exception to this apparent indifference was in the matter of his dog. Mr Gotobed had several jobs, gathering and ordering the scant woodlands in the neithbourhood, and, to each one, he took his old blind dog along with him. They had a kind of partnership in which they divided up their available incapacities and struggled through the wind and the rain with them. It was the source of much local gossip, and there was lively curiosity bordering on gambling, in the village, as to which of the two would pass away first.

Father, however, in his capacity as vicar, took it upon himself to tell Mr Gotobed to have his dog put down. In the words of the local postmistress, 'The old man went spare.' In retaliation, the dog in question was forbidden to enter the rectory gates. Our gardener had tried smuggling him in once or twice, on summer days, but he had been banished and insulted in such a way that he never forgave my father. Rather than turn the other cheek, Mr Gotobed devised a way of getting his own back. This he did by smuggling a live tortoise – Fred – into the garden, and giving it to me as a pet.

There were some rough bits at the end of the grounds which had once formed a paddock, and it was here that Fred lived, hidden from the parochial pogroms. I could never have managed without Mr Gotobed's silent, but expert, help. Four times a year, on the solstice and the equinox, Father would lay traps and bait for any recalcitrant members of the animal kingdom rash enough to imagine they had a sanctuary within the metal fences of our grounds. Four times a year, Mr Gotobed, who was party to these purges, would scoop up Fred and hide him in his pocket, and then return him when it was safe to do so. He protected Fred for me during my school terms, and he trained him to stay within the confines of the paddock where the long grass camouflaged him.

All through my bachelor days, Fred lived with me, hibernating in a wooden box during the winter and spring terms, and behind a battered chesterfield sofa during the summer in my digs. He came with me through my most reckless affairs, and through all my upheavals. By the time I had settled down in Tanza Road, he had come to be the living symbol of my past. He was the good that came out of evil. As I worried and thought and philosophized through my youth, Fred remained calm and unrushable under his thickening shell. When I practised gathering symbols, that tortoise was a repository of potential meanings. I often thought of your tale of how Aeschylus had been killed by an eagle dropping a tortoise on his head. I felt that if I puzzled away for long enough, I would find some hidden meaning in those words. So I was the worrier, the poet and thinker, and you were the eagle, and Fred, obviously, was the tortoise.

I know that you don't remember it, but it really felt that you had dropped him on my head in Larenguebec. I never knew, while you were away there, that you had even taken Fred with you. He was, after all, my tortoise. We had never been possessive about things, but Fred was Fred. Long before I went out to Larenguebec, Mrs King had her obsession about the disappearing tortoise, and it really seemed as though he had just wandered off into the unnatural heat of that summer and might still wander back one day, later. On the beach, when I discovered that you had taken him in the pram and forgotten him there, it was just too much for me. Coming back and having Mrs King going on about him, when I had other losses to mourn, was more than I could bear.

Subsequently, I have felt guilty about just leaving his remains where I found them, under the compartment of Amadeo's pram. Looking back, though, I had been burying all night, and dealing

137

with disasters, and to find him there too was like a condolence note with a 'P.S. Your cat is dead' on it. The cat was actually alive and well and one of the few creatures to benefit from the whole episode. Back in London, I found it impossible to think normally again with Mrs King winding me up daily. I thought, if only she would ask about the cat or the twins, then I could say, truthfully, that I felt they were fine.

I wanted to know what made you and me so different from other people that we should be visited by such calamity. I wanted to know why what was normal for others had tipped over the knife edge for us and become macabre. Was it because you were a star? I didn't know. You used to say that everybody had a star in them, it was just a matter of letting it show. Maybe, it was because we were so much in love, maybe that was unnatural; but you would point out stray couples at bus stops or in the street or on park benches, and you'd say that they were probably just as much in love as we were. There is something universal about some things, you said; but I would lie awake at night and think 'Why me?' Why should I have a child buried in an unmarked grave? Why should our life be marked out for this grief? Why should I have to hide like this?

You had a calmness in you, Rosalind, that I couldn't understand. I just saw my own predicament, as the one who knew, and I grew to be afraid of my own shadow. I thought, if only I didn't know, I could be happy. If I didn't know about the filled pit in the sand, and Fred, stinking to high heaven, abandoned in his pram, I could relax and live my life.

When we finally left Tanza Road, and came back out here to Sestri Levante, I was nearly out of my mind with worry. Two years had passed since your trip to France. It was seven school holidays since your illness and Amadeo's death, seven half-terms, but it seemed like yesterday to me. By the time we left, Mrs King had long since ceased to work for us, yet I still tortured myself imagining what would happen if she and Candy were to tell their differing tales. When the twins broke up from school, I felt my adrenalin run berserk each time they opened their mouths to speak to you or to strangers. They had never mentioned Amadeo again except to me,

138

and even then it was just to tell me that you would be upset if his name were to be spoken. It was as though they had inherited your ability to forget. After that, you set the tone and they followed you. You cleared his nursery, and they never looked for it again.

Everybody had grown to live with their grief, except for me, and mine was eating out my time. Then, after we moved, and sold the house in Tanza Road, there seemed to be nothing left to disturb me. I didn't even need to deal with the sale, because we did it by proxy from Italy through an estate agent. All we had to do was to sign a few bits of paper at a lawyer's office in Sestri, and then send the documents back to London by train. That sale was as painless as the occasion, ten years before, when we ourselves had bought it.

For a time, it looked as though my extended autopsy on the events at Larenguebec and their possible consequences were to be eclipsed by the much more mundane worry of finding somewhere to live. It felt very important to me that we be in Sestri Levante itself. I suppose, because I was freelance and doing fairly well, and you had long since stopped acting but could go back at any time, we were relatively free to live wherever we chose. Having the twins at school in Switzerland, with a special facility provided by Miss Juniper's loyal and efficient staff of escorting the girls on and off aeroplanes, meant that they could come and be with us anywhere.

When we discussed where we might go, you told me to choose the place where I would feel most relaxed, and that you would find a way of being happy there. At first, I almost resented your inner ease. I felt that it was unjust that I alone should suffer in the way I did for something that had happened to us both, or, if anything, had been worse for you than for me. Yet it seemed, on reflection, that you had discovered something at Sestri Levante all those years before on our honeymoon. The more I thought about the place, and about the two bays, and about the vision of Angelo on the water, the more I longed for my own initiation into the strange world of calm you now lived in, where you seemed to accept everything that had happened.

So I chose for us to return to the Italian Riviera, to the Liguria, with its 'Five Lands' and its beaches and the peninsula of Sestri with its two bays; its two faces, as they refer to it inland. For the first few weeks we stayed in a hotel up on the hill overlooking the Bay of

Silence, nestled under the lower terraces of the monastery garden. You set yourself the task of finding a house or flat for us to rent or buy, and I set out to find my angel of redemption. Although you said that some things were universal, dreams are not always shared. Even you found that out, when you started traipsing around the agents, asking about places to live. Some of them told you of places where the noughts on the rentals seemed to have trailed into the infinite, making the millions of lire become thousands of millions and beyond the range even of prematurely retired film stars like yourself. Others told you that there was nowhere available, and still others dragged you round tiny, windowless rooms and insisted that there was nothing else, or ever would be, 'not in Sestri'.

You have always been able to deal with disaster, and somehow or other to save yourself from trials far beyond the natural endurance of most human beings. I know that women are supposed to be tougher than men at bearing crises. So it's strange that really minor things can crumble your world away for you. A rude word in a shop or a brusque estate agent can still reduce you to tears. Perhaps that is what our partnership is: to share our loads, each to the best of our ability. And my abilities are in the mundane chores, while yours are in a higher, wider sphere.

I had been making my own search, largely by spending hours in the various churches of the town, and by haunting the railway station. I got to know every line of graffiti in the underground tunnel that linked the two halves of the town on either side of its tracks. I also became an expert on the interior of the church of Santa Maria di Nazareth. I thought that if I looked long enough at the plaster images and the dripping candles and the painted shrines, something would come to me, and ease my mind, and save me from the memory of Larenguebec. I sat for so many hours on the same wooden seat in the same place of that church each day, that the parish priest came and spoke to me. First of all, he asked me if I was troubled; then if I wanted to convert; and thirdly whether I was planning to stay long. I felt vaguely tempted to follow your faith, but I knew that there was a difference between yours and theirs. I had grown up in a stark world devoid of ritual and mysticism, and the sheer richness of Catholicism appealed to me.

There was something in me, though, that linked my father's hands to the hands of this priest. I joined them in a communal narrowness that I wanted to escape from. It felt like, for all its kindliness, the same narrowness that had burnt heretics at the stake. I reasoned with myself that, since what I most liked was the building and its music and its candles and lights, I could appreciate them all as a tourist can. I felt vulnerable. I think you said that it was Voltaire who on his deathbed was invited to renounce the devil, and who replied that he felt, in his present, weak state, it would be a bad time to make such a new and powerful enemy. I suppose I felt a bit like that.

Then you came, and found me staring up at the ceiling with nothing but a crick in my neck for my pains, and you begged me to help you find a house. As soon as I took the strain from you, Rosalind, you found one yourself. Things are often like that, I've noticed. I took the responsibility of dealing with everyone, while you waited for me, in coffee bars. So, after a few days of house-hunting, in which I came up with nothing but was not unduly upset by it, I went to meet you at a bar overlooking the sea. You were sitting out on the terrace, in the March wind, with your cappuccino grown cold, talking to a woman in Italian. You introduced us and I thought nothing of it, until, two weeks of solid searching later, you came up with this splendid flat between the two of you – a whole floor in a palace stuccoed with peeling frescoes and looking out directly over the Bay of Silence.

Between sorting out the workmen and helping you to arrange and repair the furniture that got damaged in transit from London, I still spent a lot of time at the station. I worked out the different shifts of all the officials there, and I have grown more acquainted with the ticket and customs staff than I am with any of our neighbours. Each time I saw the back of a grey uniform, I waited with a kind of hanging expectation for the face to turn, and to see Angelo's grey eyes, Amadeo's grey eyes, and for them to explain to me where I went wrong. When I wasn't there or at a church, I would sit or stand for hours staring out to sea, trying desperately to see what you can see when you stare like that. I hardly saw you during that time. I used to walk through the crack between the two worlds, and feel my own head seem to want to burst.

141

When I did see you, I saw your fragility and I wanted to protect it, and I saw your strength and I wanted to learn how to share it. Then I saw Rosalind Palliser, the actress, and more and more, I failed to see you. I spent a whole afternoon sitting in the church at the end of the square, and I could see that a section of the daily visitors there found my presence disturbing. I was doggedly determined to relax, and so I ignored their stares and advances. I had pills to unwind me, but I've taken too many pills. I don't like the way I feel with them any more. I want to feel something real for myself, and nothing is going to deter me. I felt my joints and back ache from sitting still so tensely for so long, and I walked back to our flat stiffly. There's a front and a back entrance. I was going to the front one, when I noticed a pretty light on the sea.

I realize, that despite staring at it for hours and hours, I haven't really noticed the light on the sea before. I followed through the thin alleyway that joined the bay to the town, and I watched the twilight hovering on the water. It was coming up for seven o'clock. There's always a mass at seven and I've come to vacate the church just before it, to avoid the stares and whispers of the parish. I heard the bells ringing behind me, and, for once, I felt that they weren't ringing to complain or appeal. Nor were they yet ringing to test your memory, it seemed that they were just ringing, and they sounded very natural in the oncoming night. I walked past the fishing boats on the sand, and I saw you standing half-way along the beach. You were picking up glass, and you didn't see me. There is a wealth of green sea glass in the sand and you have jars of it in the flat.

As I walked towards you, I began to feel relaxed for the first time in two years. Something in me dragged instinctively back, and made my mind rush for a moment to see what I should do. The boats were in place and they were not mine. The beach was empty. The bells were ringing, but I'd just been to church and I didn't need to go again; you were not asking anything of me, nobody was. I, William Walsh, the vicar's son, was flaying my own back, mortifying my own flesh to atone for something that you hadn't done. Then the light grew dimmer, and you stood up and smiled at me.

All the time that I was looking for a way to rest, I didn't realize that the way was always there. I never blamed you for anything, Rosalind, because I knew that you had done your best. Well, I did

142

too. I think you always knew that; even behind your denial of facts, you knew that we were just two people struggling through, and we did what we could and we couldn't do more, so you had no regrets. I picked up bits of coloured sea glass with you that evening, and I felt that with each piece I gathered I was gathering back another bit of my sanity. We stayed there until long after it was dark, picking up what seemed like our shattered stock of life, and I felt the rhythm and the calm of the sea heal me, not by my willing or wanting it to, but because we were both there.

There was a seagull suspended in the air over the sea, hovering with its grey wings like eyes. I stared at it almost unconsciously. I noticed, when I paused, that you were staring at it too. We stayed there until the night grew cold. Finally I said, 'There was a man once who lost half an hour every morning and ran after it all the rest of the day, without being able to overtake it.' I rearranged my shoulders to fit the Italian waiter I used to be, then I said, 'Well, I've stopped doing that now.'

Bel Mooney
The Anderson Question £2.95

Bel Mooney was born and brought up in Liverpool. As a philosophy student at London University, she met her future husband, the broadcaster Jonathan Dimbleby. They now live near Bath with their son and daughter. THE WINDSURF BOY, her first novel, reached the *Sunday Times* bestseller list. Bel Mooney has worked as a journalist for a wide variety of publications and has appeared regularly on television and radio. She is now a regular columnist on the *Sunday Times*, and reviews fiction for *Cosmopolitan*.

Eleanor Anderson's comfortable and well-ordered life is completely shattered when her husband David, the dependable and much respected village doctor, disappears. A few days later he is found dead, apparently the victim of a heart attack, and speculation is stilled as family, friends and patients alike feel a kind of relief at knowing the worst.

But genuine grief at their bereavement gives way to angry bewilderment when a post-mortem reveals that the man they thought they knew so well, the man they all depended on, had taken his own life, for no obvious reason. And Eleanor discovers, in the uneasy company of her ungracious son, that all she had assumed and lived by has been false . . .

'Beautifully written, compassionate . . . extremely moving . . . one of the best novels I have read for a long time' *Books and Bookmen*

All these books are available at your local bookshop or newsagent, or can be ordered direct from the publisher. Indicate the number of copies required and fill in the form below

. . . .

Name ————————————————————————————
(Block letters please)

Address ————————————————————————————

————————————————————————————————————

Send to CS Department, Pan Books Ltd,
PO Box 40, Basingstoke, Hants
Please enclose remittance to the value of the cover price plus:
60p for the first book plus 30p per copy for each additional book
ordered to a maximum charge of £2.40 to cover postage and
packing
Applicable only in the UK

While every effort is made to keep prices low, it is sometimes
necessary to increase prices at short notice. Pan Books reserve the
right to show on covers and charge new retail prices which may
differ from those advertised in the text or elsewhere